OUR DARKNESS, HIS LIGHT

ORDINARY PEOPLE IN THE EXTRAORDINARY STORY OF CHRIST

BRUCE HENNIGAN

hope**again**
books

Printed in the United States of America

Published by Hope Again Books

An Imprint of LifeFilters, LLC

All Bible verses are in the New International Version translation and are included by permission of the publisher.

Book Cover Design by ebooklaunch.com

❦ Created with Vellum

To every person who participated in the drama ministry at Brookwood Baptist Church — Good Show! Our spotlight always illuminated the cross!

TRUE LIGHT

The people walking in **darkness** have seen a great **light**; on those living in the land of **deep darkness** a **light** has dawned.
  Isaiah 9:2 (NIV)

* * *

In the beginning was the Word, and the Word was with God, and the Word was God. He was with God in the beginning. Through him all things were made; without him nothing was made that has been made. In him was life, and that life was the **light** of all mankind. The **light** shines in the **darkness**, and the **darkness** has not overcome it.

The **true light** that gives **light** to everyone was coming into the world. He was in the world, and though the world was made through him, the world did not recognize him. He came to that which was his own, but his own did not receive him. Yet to all who did receive him, to those who believed in his name, he gave the right to become children of God— children born not of *natural descent, nor of human decision or a husband's will, but born of God.*

John 1:1-5;9-13 (NIV)

INTRODUCTION

What did the innkeeper think when shepherds showed up at his manger?

Who owned the "colt" that carried Jesus on his triumphant entry into Jerusalem?

Who made the bowl Jesus used to wash the disciples' feet?

Who carried the basin in which Pilate washed his hands?

Who were the two thieves on either side of Jesus at the crucifixion?

We do not know. But, it is certain these people were ordinary citizens of Judea living out their ordinary lives almost two thousand years ago. They had no idea they were becoming a part of the greatest Story ever told!

For fifteen years I had the privilege of being in charge of the drama ministry of Brookwood Baptist Church. During that time, my pastor, Mark Sutton, asked me to write many short dramas based on scripture as accompanying illustrations for his sermons. I became fascinated with these "ordinary" people around Jesus. These everyday people going about their innocuous lives would find themselves pulled into extraordinary circumstances and found themselves involved in the Story to end all Stories!

As the director of the drama ministry I found myself performing all kinds of duties: Producer, director, actor, playwright, costume maker, running sound, programming lights, working backstage, cooking snacks. You name it, I had to do it at one time or another and this taught me a powerful lesson. When the main "star" is on the stage delivering the story of the play, there are dozens of unseen people behind the scenes who made that moment possible. They never see the spotlight and rarely stand center stage. But their contributions are necessary so the "star" of the show can make sure the Story is told!

Jesus Christ is center stage of all time and space. He chose those who worked "backstage" because of their own individual stories, their talents, their skills, their inborn purpose and spiritual gifts. They all played an important and integral part in the overall Story of Redemption. And, Jesus saw what C. S. Lewis wrote about in his book "The Weight of Glory":

> "There are no ordinary people. You have never talked to a mere mortal. Nations, cultures, arts, civilisations—these are mortal, and their life is to ours as the life of a gnat. But it is immortals whom we joke with, work with, marry, snub, and exploit—immortal horrors or everlasting splendours. . . . Next to the Blessed Sacrament itself, your neighbour is the holiest object presented to your senses. If he is your Christian neighbour, he is holy in almost the same way, for in him also Christ vere latitat—the glorifier and the glorified, Glory Himself, is truly hidden."

This book tells the stories of those "backstage", "ordinary" people who were suddenly and surprisingly thrust into the limelight as they played a part in the greatest Story ever told. These seemingly insignificant people swirled around the events of the life of the Prince of Peace from the crowded streets of

Bethlehem to the empty tomb. Each person was an intended part of the Story – in their pain, their weakness, their failings, their flaws, their darkness. These ordinary people were a part of the Story God was unfolding, the nexus of redemption, the center of all of time and space coming into focus on the cross. Who were these people? Who made room in the inn for a pregnant girl? Who asked Jesus about taxes? Who carved the bowl Jesus used to wash his disciples' feet? Who owned the rooster that signaled to Peter his greatest failure?

In this book, truly fictional, I have asked that question and imagined an answer. I do not know if the people you will meet in this book really experienced the circumstances used by God to complete the crucial chapter of the Greatest Story Ever Told. But I do know that God used them for His glorious purposes and in using them, He made them grow, made them see a glimmer of a Bigger Picture. In allowing them to fulfill their purposes in their roles in the Story, God gave them a taste of eternal water!

This work is one of imagination. But it is woven into the fabric of Truth. Truth incarnate. Truth in person. Truth nailed to a cross and dying for our lies. Each person partaking of this Story was unaware of their part in God's Story. Although this work is parable based on truth, it illustrates the potential stories of US; of those who found themselves pulled into the death and resurrection of God incarnate.

And, each person could not imagine how their brokenness, their failures, their darkness could lead to His light. The stage is dark, the Script filled with gaps and holes; waiting; groaning to be Complete. Each hole, each emptiness in God's Story has a perfect role that must be filled. He invites US to fill those roles. We are standing in the shadows of this world ruled by the Enemy looking for reasons, for explanations, for a light to shine into the shadows. Perhaps it is only in the shadows we can see our place in the Story. The darkness is OUR darkness. The darkness comes from OUR brokenness. And, the darkness is already defeated!

Pause now and look about you in the shadows. Look about you for the work of God as He pulls you into Completion, into His Story. We are not destined to stay in our broken state. We are not destined to dwell forever in our darkness. It is only in the dark that we truly appreciate the Light. For, in our darkness, we, along with the world, will see His light!

Bruce Hennigan
November, 2020

CHAPTER 1

THE LIGHT IN THE DARKNESS

So Joseph also went up from the town of Nazareth in Galilee to Judea, to Bethlehem the town of David, because he belonged to the house and line of David. He went there to register with Mary, who was pledged to be married to him and was expecting a child. While they were there, the time came for the baby to be born, and she gave birth to her firstborn, a son. She wrapped him in cloths and placed him in a manger, because there was no guest room available for them.
Luke 2:4-7 (NIV)

I heard my wife gasping for breath as she climbed the ladder to the upper level of our home. "Rachel, you should be in bed." I growled.

"Josiah, you were the one who let them use the manger."

"They didn't have much money, but what else could I do? The father is my distant cousin. You agreed to let the other room to your sister and her family." I pointed to the meager dividing wall that separated our living area from the other room on the second level of our home. I could hear all five of her relatives snoring. "The other inns were full. I couldn't turn away an expectant mother. I saw too much of you in her desperate eyes."

Rachel groaned as she lowered herself to her sleeping mat and rubbed her stomach. "I know, I know. She was pregnant, like me. Only, I have two more months."

"And, you have the skills of a midwife." I said.

"A midwife who is very large and very tired." Rachel sighed.

"And, what of the baby?" I asked.

"I know it will surprise you, but he helped deliver the child. I was there so they would not have to go through that alone. I am glad you stayed away." Rachel said.

"You know the law." I said. I could not afford to be "unclean" if I was to go to the synagogue in the coming days. I listened to the gentle crying of the baby from the manger below. "I could have sent them away. But when my cousin said his name was Joseph." I paused and emotion cracked my voice.

Rachel reached out and touched my arm. "I did not know."

I glanced at her stomach. "When our son is born, we will name him after my brother."

Rachel jerked her hand away and covered her mouth. "No! We are having a daughter and we will name her Sybil."

I felt the old anger stoke. We had been through this many times. "God is giving us a son and we will name him in honor of my brother."

Rachel's eyes filled with the inevitable fire. "And, will our son also be a rebel? Will he join the ranks of the crucified?"

I looked away from her. "No! I will raise him differently. He will not sacrifice himself on a cross in a vain effort to defeat the Romans."

Rachel turned her back to me and reclined on her mat. "I will not argue with you tonight about this, Josiah. A new life has entered our home and this child is special. Our child will be a special daughter. You will see."

I stood up, my anger and rage taking me. "I said he will be known as Joseph!" I hurried across the small bedroom to the ladder leading to the roof.

"Where are you going?" Rachel said harshly.

"To cool my fevered brow." I snapped. I climbed the ladder and stepped out onto the roof of my house. The night was unbearably clear with a million glittering stars winking in the black velvet sky. One star in the west seemed unusually close and strikingly bright. I settled onto a wooden bench and studied the dwindling crowds hurrying into their crowded homes with the coming of the darkness. The Roman census was upon us and towns swelled with strangers and travelers. Ah, the cursed Romans!

I looked up from the torch lit streets and gazed toward the hills. That way lay Jerusalem. The couple in the manger with their newborn child said they had come from Nazareth which in itself was a long journey. But, to come from Jerusalem would take weeks. I could faintly make out the rippling distant mountains. It was upon one of those ridges along a Roman road they had crucified my brother, Joseph.

The hothead would not listen to reason! I warned him not to rebel against the Romans. But he joined in with hundreds of men protesting the Roman occupation. And, he had paid for his life with the cruelest form of death known to man. For a while, my people had hoped our king, Herod, would stand up for us against the Romans. But Herod was a mere puppet, left in power only if he kept the populace under control. There had been many crucifixions lately. Herod had proven to be worse than the Romans!

Yahweh had promised a redeemer, a king to bring an end to our suffering. When would he come? When would we be delivered from this daily life of bitter pain and suffering? The anger and pain took me and I fell to my knees praying to Yahweh for peace. Would that peace ever come? Would this world ever be free from strife and discord?

"My son, you must walk with me." A voice echoed in my mind. I stood up and glanced around the rooftop. It was empty. Who had spoken? The voice had such depth and power to it. I should have been terrified. But, instead, a growing sense of tranquility soothed my beating heart.

Against all reason, I felt the desire to walk. Yahweh would protect those living in my inn. I felt certain of that. Normally, I would take the walk in the daytime. The next day would be one year since my brother had died. But, now, reassured by God in a strange sense of temporary peace, I decided it was time to take my annual walk up the mountain.

The road on the mountain side wound its way past Bethlehem toward the distant city of Jerusalem. They say the Roman roads connected every city in the empire to Rome. All roads led to Rome. And, they say the Romans brought us a more civilized, advanced way of living. But, the cost of that way of life was at the expense of their terrible cruelty.

I paused at the top of the winding walking path and stared at the road before me. Rocks were carefully pressed together to make a smooth surface over which the Romans could bring their chariots, wagons, and marching hordes of soldiers. I stepped out onto its surface. The sky was afire with a million stars. The one bright star I had seen from my rooftop continued to gleam and glisten in the ebon skies. It cast its light on the empty road. I stood in the middle of this instrument of civilization, this gift to our "backward" people.

I looked out over the small village of Bethlehem. I could see my inn near the edge and for a moment, I thought I heard the distant cry of the newborn baby. I turned back to the road and crossed to the far side. In the meager star light, I searched the ground. Where was it? There it was!

I squatted beside a cluster of rocks and reached out to touch the rough decaying wooden stump shoved deeply into the earth. I ran my hand over the splinters and drew a deep breath as one of them pierced my skin. My blood dripped onto the timber, joining the blood of my brother. This is where they had crucified him. This is where the Romans had made an "example" of dozens of my friends including my hot-headed zealot of a brother.

"Why?" I studied the blood dripping from my finger. "Why did you have to die? Why did you have to shed your blood for our people? Don't you see how useless it was?" My hand formed a fist and I stood up as anger surged through my mind. The peace I had felt on my rooftop had quickly evaporated in the face of my anger. I turned and howled at the empty sky.

"Why, Yahweh, why? Why have you forsaken your people? Why did you let Joseph die on this cross at the hands of these Gentiles? When will you come? When will you send your Messiah to rescue us?" Tears ran down my cheek as my shouts echoed through the canyons and died out in the night.

And then, I heard it. The voices were ethereal, unearthly and musical without being music. I whirled and looked through the empty space where once my brother had hung on a cross. The sound came from over the hilltop and light began to grow beyond the ridge. I stepped over the stump of my brother's cross and made my way up the rocky slope. As I grew nearer to the top of the hill, the voices grew louder washing over me, filling my mind and my heart with awe. What was this?

The light seemed fluid, flowing around me like a gentle stream in a soft rainstorm. I topped the hill with my breath tearing through my lungs, my heart pounding and gazed down in wonder at the shepherds standing on the hill beneath me. Their gaze was turned upward even as mine had been when I had shouted angrily at Yahweh. But what they saw!

The sky was filled with them; thousands and thousands of beings of pure light and glistening robes and faces filled with wonder and, yes, joy! Their voices filled the air like incense. I inhaled it. I bathed in it. I longed for it.

"Glory to God in the highest, and on earth peace, good will toward men." The words filled my mind. And with them, the peace returned, a joy that flooded my wounded heart. The depression and despair that just moments ago had swathed me in a cloud of smothering darkness was blown away like dust by the song of the angels. I fell to my knees. Peace? Could such a thing come? Joy? Would I feel joy again? Good will toward men? Did that mean even the Romans? Even Herod?

One of the beings of light descended to the shepherds. The angel was with them, but it was suddenly with me, standing before me in all of its glory. I drank in the celestial light and love. I sobbed with the joy of the touch of the divine. The angel's face beamed and it spoke without speaking.

"Fear not: for, behold, I bring you good tidings of great joy, which shall be to all people. For unto you is born this day in the city of David a Saviour, which is Christ the Lord. And this shall be a sign unto you; You shall find the babe wrapped in swaddling clothes, lying in a manger." The angel leaned toward me. "In a manger."

I fell back and covered my face in shame. In a manger? Could it be? Had the Messiah indeed come to us? But, in my manger? Born among animals and filth? My animals? My filth? I rolled onto my stomach and sobbed into the dry earth. What had I done? I had cursed Yahweh! I had shaken my fist at Him! I had demanded He do something to relieve me of my suffering. But it was not supposed to be like this. The Messiah was a king, a conqueror who should have been born in the palace of the high king. Instead, he was born in a manger! In MY manger!

I rolled over and the night had once again darkened. I heard a scraping, scratching sound and suddenly the sheep from the hillside were all about me, running, jumping, leaping in joy as they tore over the hilltop and descended toward Bethlehem. The shepherds followed. One stopped and reached out a hand.

"Will you join us? Will you come and see this thing which has come to pass that the Lord has made known to us." His face was bright with joy.

I looked at his rough, calloused hand. I grimaced at his odor of night and sweat and sheep. I reached out and took his hand.

"Yes. I know where this thing has taken place. In a manger."

The shepherd smiled. "Yes. The Lamb of God would only be born in a manger."

He walked past me, leaving me standing alone on the hilltop as he followed the other shepherds and their sheep down into the sleeping town of Bethlehem. He had come that night. He had come in a way I could never anticipate. Yahweh worked in ways I could not understand!

I felt the blood trickle down my hand from the wound in my finger. For a moment, my depression lifted; my despair vanished in the realization that the Messiah had come! My brother would be avenged.

And then, a creeping oppression fell over me. I looked long and hard at the blood on my hand. I felt the splinters of the cross. In a flash, I saw the future, a vision that could only come from Yahweh and realized that as painful as it was to have seen my brother die on a cross, it was nothing compared with what lay ahead for the Messiah. I made my way down the hill side and stepping over my bother's cross, over the past which I could no longer change. I embraced Yahweh's future for us all.

CHAPTER 2

THE GIFTS

After Jesus was born in Bethlehem in Judea, during the time of King Herod, Magi from the east came to Jerusalem and asked, "Where is the one who has been born king of the Jews? We saw his star when it rose and have come to worship him."

Matthew 2:1-2 (NIV)

"Where are you going?" Rachel asked.

I shrugged into my outer cloak and grabbed the walking stick. "I promised Joseph I would help him finish something in his workshop." I couldn't tell her it was a chair I was making especially for her.

My son, Joseph, burbled and cooed in his mother's arms. "But, it's after sunset."

"Yes, and much cooler. Joseph's workshop on his roof will be much more tolerable now." I kissed my son's forehead. His dark, unruly hair smelled of scented oil. "You know, it's been two years." I tousled Joseph's hair and he grabbed my finger with his strong grip.

"Since the birth of Yeshua. Yes, I remember, Josiah. Also, that was the night we had our, uh, disagreement."

I reached past Joseph and patted Rachel's stomach. "And, this child will be our daughter, Rachel. Yahweh has told me as much."

Rachel's smile was brighter than the star I had seen that night. "Well, I will be putting our Joseph down for the night so be careful on your journey to Joseph's house." She leaned forward and kissed me on the cheek.

I stepped out of our house into the cool night air. The sky was clear and filled with blazing stars. One star in particular seemed to lie low on the horizon. For two years now, the star had filled the night sky visible even with a full moon! Now, it seemed brighter and closer than ever! As I turned toward Joseph's house, I noticed the star seemed to hover over the street where he lived! How was this possible? Surely just an illusion.

Warm, moist air bathed the back of my neck and I whirled. Moisture hit me on the cheek! My eyes widened as I stared into the snout of a camel. I stumbled back in shock. Astride the camel sat the most unusual man I had ever seen. His robes were shiny and shimmering in the star light. A golden colored turban covered his head and his long, gray beard was dotted with gold chain woven into the hairs. More camels appeared at his side. Another notable individual came into sight.

The man wore a long, dark crimson robe embroidered with shiny silver threads. His deep crimson turban was swept up into a peak and his long, black beard bore hanging pearls. He was tall in the seat of his camel and he grimaced at my sight.

"Camel spit is good for you, my friend." He said in a heavy accent.

A third man astride a camel was short and dumpy and dressed in resplendent white and copper. His flat turban sat on his head like a plate. His white beard and mustache matched his outfit. He laughed.

"Our friend is not accustomed to camels, it seems. My good friend, we have come a long way looking for the King. Can you tell us where to find him?" The white clad man asked.

"We follow the star." The first man said pointing to the shining star in the distance.

"For two years we have followed the star!" The crimson clad man growled.

"Yes, but tonight it is most assuredly bright, and it has come to rest. I believe our days of following the star may be over. After all, King Herod's seers agreed with our assessment." Gold said.

I looked behind them at a long entourage of camels and men filling the meager streets of Bethlehem. People had emerged from their homes and talked among themselves.

"Who are you?" I asked.

"We are magi from the East. We saw the signs in the heavens predicted by your prophet Daniel. They told of the birth of the King of Kings. Maybe two years ago? We are not certain if the signs appeared at his conception or at his birth, but he would be between one and two years of age." White said.

"Signs in the heavens?" I said hoarsely. Like angels singing? Like shepherds visiting my manger? "I think I know of who you speak. But he is no king. He is the son of a carpenter, born in my meager manger. No fanfare. No royal reception. I cannot say that he is a king."

White laughed. "See, I told you we should have paid more attention to the writings of Isaiah! He described a lowly birth for the king among commoners." He looked at me. "There was one seer in an ebon black robe who insisted this king would be born in a palace. His icy blue eyes were particularly piercing, and he had Herod's ear. My friends were almost persuaded, but I have studied the prophecies. I believe this king will be a servant leader, not necessarily a commander of armies. I believe he will surprise everyone with his nature as a king. But my partners disagree."

"He will be a mighty priest king!" Gold pronounced.

"He will be a sacrifice for his people." White spoke. "His love for his people will be so great, he will give his life in service to his people."

I shook my head. "I do not know of what you speak. Our scriptures talk of the Messiah, the coming conqueror who will free us."

"There are those who still subscribe to such a theory." Gold said.

"Like Herod's seers?" Crimson said. "I do not trust them. Fear filled their eyes when we spoke of the star."

"Fear of Herod!" White said. "Everyone knows how ruthless the man can be."

I pointed toward the star. "If what you suspect is true, that star is over my friend's house. He has a young boy just now two years old." My heart began to race. Could it be true? Was Yeshua the Messiah? If so, I hoped and prayed he was none of these magi's visions for a king. The Messiah would rescue us from the Romans. And, from Herod. And, get vengeance for the death of my brother! "I will take you there."

What followed was the strangest parade Bethlehem had ever seen. We reached the street that led to Joseph's small house. "There." I pointed. Crimson motioned to a nearby empty field. "Set up our tents there." He spoke to servants behind him. "In the morning we will present our tribute to the king."

"Set up your tents if you will." Gold slid off of his camel. "But, I am seeing the king tonight! We have journeyed too far to sit idly during the night." He clapped his hands and one of his servants ran forward with a golden box. "I suggest the two of you get your gifts ready. I am sure the boy will be asleep soon."

I ran to Joseph's house and knocked on his door. The

latched clicked open and Joseph smiled when he saw me. "Josiah, I was hoping you had not forgotten. We finish the chair tonight."

Behind him in the soft glow from a lamp, Yeshua sat on the floor in a white robe. He played with two sheep Joseph had carved from wood. Mary stood up from her chair. Her face stiffened. "What is it, Josiah? You look frightened."

"It is the magi. They have followed the star. They are looking for a king." I mumbled and from behind me I heard the sudden harmonious cacophony of a dozen voices raised in chanting. Joseph and Mary moved past me and I stepped into the room. Yeshua stood up and reached out to take my robe in his hands. He looked up at me with the most intense gaze and his long, brown hair curled around his ears.

"It's okay, little one. They mean no harm."

But Yeshua did not seem frightened. He seemed expectant? Waiting? Fulfilled? I could not adequately describe the expression on his toddler face. He turned to the open door and walked forward, pausing just within the frame.

Gold spoke with Joseph and Mary and his voice carried into the house. "We spoke to Herod's seers and they told us according to your scripture:

'In Bethlehem in Judea you will find him. For this is what the prophet has written:

'But you, Bethlehem, in the land of Judah, are by no means least among the rulers of Judah; for out of you will come a ruler who will shepherd my people Israel.' We have traveled from the East for long months to see this new king."

Mary reached to Joseph and he pulled her into his embrace. "We knew something like this might happen." Joseph said. "Gabriel came to me in a dream."

"And, spoke to me in person." Mary said. They both turned and looked at Yeshua standing in the doorway. Their faces were lit up by a combination of awe, and yes, fear. Gold's face paled and he stepped forward with the golde box. He knelt before the child.

"I bring you a gift of gold. It is the gift to a king. May your reign bring peace to our world." He placed the golden box at the boy's feet.

Crimson came forward and knelt beside his companion. "I bring you the gift of Frankincense, the offering of a priest for the righteousness of his people. May your reign be filled with compassion and forgiveness." He placed a wooden box with silver highlights before the boy.

White came forward and his face was stained with tears. His mouth was trembling and he knelt before the boy. He held out a pure, white urn with a flat top. "And, with a heart broken by the prophecies I bring you myrrh, the herb used to anoint the dead. For, if you are the king the prophets truly foretell, you will give all for those you love." He placed the receptacle before the boy.

* * *

THE VISIT of the Magi was the talk of the town for days while they camped in the nearby foothills. Once they had worshipped Yeshua, they had retired to their tents to rest before their long trip back through Jerusalem and to their Eastern lands. Rachel and Joseph were on the roof when I got up that morning. She held Joseph and was pointing to the tents in the distance.

"Those are camels. And they live in those beautiful tents, Joseph. They are strangers to this land."

Joseph laughed and clapped his hands. I placed a hand on the boy's hair and ruffled it. "My son, I love you so much."

Joseph looked up at me. "Da?"

My heart swelled with pride. I raised my arms and stretched them out as far as they would go. "I love you this much and more than I can reach."

Joseph looked at his own hands and then stretched them out

13

as far as he could. "Da!" He smiled.

I turned away from Rachel to hide my tears of joy. But when my gaze fell on the tents I felt my heart tremble with the news I had learned. "They will soon return to Jerusalem. I was told by one of the servants that Herod requested they give him a report." I frowned. "I'm not so sure that is a good idea."

Rachel glared at me. "Why would you say such?"

"The man had his wife and mother-in-law killed. And, then had his three sons executed! He does not worship Yahweh, Rachel. He has killed anyone in his way! No man in his right man would trust such a king!"

Rachel put her hands over Joseph's ears. "Must you speak thus before our son?" She pulled Joseph more tightly into her arms. He curled his bare legs over her pregnant stomach. "I'll be downstairs taking a nap with our son and future daughter." She left him standing on the roof glaring at the tents on the hillside.

* * *

THE BANGING on the door echoed through the house and Joseph woke up crying. I sat up on my mat and reached for Rachel. She was not there. She was sleeping in the other chamber with Joseph. I stumbled down the ladder to the lower level. The donkey and the goats were restless in their manger as more thudding came from the door. I opened the latch and there before me stood Joseph. Behind him astride his donkey was Mary holding Yeshua. A second donkey was burdened down with their possessions.

"Joseph?" I mumbled.

"Josiah, you are a good man. Yahweh has smiled upon you and blessed you. So, I must give you a warning. An angel of the Lord appeared to me in a dream. 'Get up,' he said, 'take the child and his mother and escape to Egypt. Stay there until I tell you, for Herod is going to search for the child to kill him.'"

My heart began to race. "But, the magi?"

"Left yesterday. I should have listened to them. One of them also had a visitation from an angel in a dream warning them not to return to their land through Jerusalem. But, Josiah, they are pagans and I did not believe an angel would visit them. Two angels have given a warning. I wanted you to know before we left. Your friendship has meant so much to me." He stepped aside and motioned to the completed chair. "I finished the chair for your wife. Go with God and have peace, my friend." He bowed his head and hurried out to Mary. He grabbed the reigns of her donkey and made his way down the street. Mary cast one long, tearful glance in my direction, and they were gone into the dark night.

I sat in the chair and looked at the sleeping city. Two angels. I had seen my own angel. No, I had seen a host of angels! Herod would kill the child? Of course, he would! This future king was a threat to his reign. The man had killed his own sons! But, how would he know which child was which? My heart froze with fear and I bolted to my feet. I looked once at the city of my childhood, the city in which I had wed my wife, the city in which my first-born son had been born and realized I would never see it again. I ran into the house to wake up Rachel. We had to leave the city, or my son Joseph would face the same fate as his late uncle.

I paused at the foot of the ladder and looked back out through the open door at the empty chair. A vision swam before me. Mothers sitting in chairs with their dead sons in their arms, wailing and weeping! I should warn them all! But they would not believe me! Who would believe such? I had no time to warn anyone. It was time to leave Bethlehem. I had a sister in Jerusalem. Perhaps she would take us in while we waited to see what Herod would do.

"Rachel, pack your bags. We must leave now!" I started up the ladder.

CHAPTER 3

THE CARPENTER'S BROTHER — PART 1

But when the Jewish Festival of Tabernacles was near, Jesus' brothers said to him, "Leave Galilee and go to Judea, so that your disciples there may see the works you do. No one who wants to become a public figure acts in secret. Since you are doing these things, show yourself to the world." For even his own brothers did not believe in him.

Therefore Jesus told them, "My time is not yet here; for you any time will do. The world cannot hate you, but it hates me because I testify that its works are evil. You go to the festival. I am not going up to this festival, because my time has not yet fully come."

John 7:2-8 (NIV)

*P*erhaps I should have been a fisherman. I looked out over the sparkling blue waters of the Sea of Galilee as some called it. I preferred Gennesaret. Maybe it was because *he* liked the other name. Yes, my brother, the prophet, the rabbi, the teacher, and according to some, the healer. I stood on the rocky slope leading down to the shores of the sea. The morning breeze carried the clean, fresh fragrance of water. The fishermen had long since come in with their catch for the day. Oh, how I hated the smell of fish!

Not far from the shore, a house stood surrounded by a crowd. The crowd was substantial. I had heard they were growing in number and following Jesus along the coast. And, he had picked his own special followers! Some of them were fisherman. But, worse, one was a tax collector. A tax collector! A collaborator with the Romans! What was he thinking? Our brother was mad, I tell you! And, now was the time to end this!

I heard footsteps behind me and my brother, Joseph paused beside me, gasping a little for breath. He was a bit overweight and not as nimble as the rest of us.

"James, mother and the others are on their way."

I raised an eyebrow. "Mother is coming? Joseph, I hoped she would stay at cousin Abraham's house."

"She insisted on seeing him." Joseph said. "James, why are we here?"

I pointed to the crowd at the water's edge. "Jesus is preaching in the house over there. And, since tomorrow is the beginning of the Feast I thought it would be a perfect time to have our talk with him."

Joseph grimaced. "I don't know about this, James. It seemed like a good idea at first. But, now?"

My brother, Simon made his way across the rocky shore. He was shorter and thinner than Joseph. He paused and glanced at us. "What seemed like a good idea?"

"He's talking about our plan, Simon." Joseph said.

Our other brother, Jude appeared at Simon's side. He was tall and well built like our father. His hands bore the callouses and muscles of a carpenter. "Brothers, I overheard. I'm beginning to have doubts."

My face burned with anger. I glared at Jude. "You are? And what of you, Simon?"

Simon glanced down the slope at the crowd around the house. "There's all those people. And, Jesus is surrounded by all of his disciples. And there are only four of us."

I drew a deep, calming breath. They were losing their nerve! "That's right. Four brothers. And at least two of his sisters. Why are you afraid of his disciples? They're just fishermen. Smelly, dirty fishermen. And, a tax collector! Look down there at the shore. See their boats? I've worked on those kinds of boats before repairing the woodwork. They stink!"

Joseph ignored me and punched Simon in the shoulder. The smaller man almost fell down. "Simon, look down there! I remember this place. Don't you?"

Simon rubbed his shoulder. "Remember? When?"

Jude crossed his arms. "Joseph is right. That's the inlet where we learned how to swim. Remember?"

"I was so young, then." Simon said. "But I seem to remember. It was the summer we came to visit cousin Abraham and I pulled up his cloak to see if father was under there."

I squinted at our smaller brother. "What?"

Simon nodded, his focus far away in the past. "Father had just passed away. And mother said he had gone to be in Abraham's bosom. So, I was looking for father. In Abraham's bosom."

I gritted my teeth. How could he be so superficial about our father's death? My heart sank at the memory of his loss.

Jude nodded. "Jesus took us out into the inlet and taught us all how to swim. Even Sarah and Rebecca."

I looked away from them at the shoreline. "He never taught me how to swim."

"You stayed behind with father to work in the carpenter shop, James. You were always busy." Joseph said.

I felt the cool breeze play over my heated face. Always, they played and laughed with him. With Jesus. Being the REAL first born, I had responsibilities. Where were they the day father died? I was with him. Right beside him while Jesus and the others were out and about. Enjoying the sunlight. Voices drifted ahead of our arriving sisters, Sarah and Rebecca.

Sarah grabbed Simon and steadied herself on the rocks. She was still young and would soon make someone a wonderful wife. Rebecca was only a year or so older and was being matched up with a son of a friend of the family. Sarah sighed and contemplated me with one of her impatient stares. "Well, we finally made it, James. Mother will be along in a moment. I hope you have a good reason for us to leave the comfort of cousin Abraham's house for this smelly seashore."

I straightened and pushed the distant memory of father's loss away. "I do have a good reason. Jesus is here and it is time we spoke to him about this matter we have discussed. I wanted all of us to be together."

"Shouldn't we wait for mother?" Rebecca said.

"No!" I said. "This is between us and Jesus. Stay here and I'll get one of his fishermen to bring him out to us."

Sarah and Rebecca looked at each other and rolled their eyes in exasperation. I could care less for their condescending attitudes. It was time to get on with this before Mother arrived. I set out across the rocky shore toward the crowd around the house. Quiet whispers and murmurs joined the gentle sound of waves lapping at the shore. And, above the susurration of the voices of the crowd, I heard HIS voice. Steady. Calm. Commanding. Always commanding! I noticed one of the fishermen moving through the crowd. I caught his eye and motioned to him.

He smiled at me. Smiled! He had no idea what I was planning. I would wipe that smile off of his face!

"I know you. You're James, Jesus's oldest brother." He offered a hand of friendly greeting and I ignored it.

"Yes. And these are his other brothers and sisters." I motioned behind me. "And you are?"

"John."

"John? Your brother's name is James, also, isn't it? And your father is Zebedee." I said.

"Yes. You know him?"

I nodded. Don't get distracted, I told myself. "I did some repair work on his boat some years back. I seem to remember that you had gone off to follow John, the Baptizer. How did you end up following Jesus?"

John smiled "He sent James and me to follow Jesus after he baptized Jesus in the Jordan River. He said that Jesus was the true Messiah about which he had been preaching. We have never regretted it."

There it was! The Messiah! How many had claimed that title in our lifetime? How many had ended up dying at the hands of our own disappointed people? I shook my head gently. "I see. Well, I wouldn't sever my ties with John if I were you. Would you please go and tell our brother we must see him?"

John's smile faded. "You haven't heard?"

"Heard what?"

"John is dead. Beheaded by Herod." John paused and pain filled his eyes. He wiped angrily at his eyes and sniffed. "But, we are to turn the other cheek, right? I'll go tell Jesus you are here." He turned and made his way through the crowd toward the house. I stepped closer and through the open door I saw *him*. He stood surrounded by all kinds of people. Women, even! John spoke to him quietly.

"Your mother and brothers are standing outside, wanting to speak to you."

Jesus looked through the open door in my direction. Our gaze met and I stood defiant and strong. He would not intimidate me! Jesus glanced around at the crowd.

"Who is my mother, and who are my brothers?" He pointed to his disciples. "Here are my mother and my brothers. For whoever does the will of my Father in heaven is my brother and sister and mother."

The words washed over me like a cold, unfeeling wave. "Anyone who hears? What of flesh and blood?" I hissed. I whirled and marched up the shore to my brothers and sisters. "Did you hear that? He won't even come over here and talk to his own brothers and sisters. Just who does he think he is?"

Our mother appeared up the hill and walked gracefully down to us. She wore a simple beige robe and her face was lined with fine wrinkles. Each wrinkle was put there by one of us, not the least of which was Jesus. She looked at each of us in the face and paused when her gaze me mine.

"James, he is his Father's son. And he must be about the business of the Father. James, I don't know what you're planning to say to Jesus, but I think we had better go back to the house."

I crossed my arms and glared right back at her. "I came here to speak to Jesus about the Feast of the Tabernacles."

Simon gasped. "Wait a minute. You didn't tell us all of your plan. Are you talking about the Feast? Do you mean in Judea?"

"Yes." I said.

Joseph towered over me. "But he said the Jews sought to kill him in Judea."

I felt a hand on my arm and looked into my mother's face. "James, surely you don't expect him to place his followers in danger?"

I would not be dissuaded by her peaceful demeanor. "There will be many followers at the Feast in Judea. He can proclaim himself in front of all of them."

Jude glanced at Rebecca and Sarah. "You mean, proclaim himself the Messiah?"

Sarah snorted. "Messiah! That's all I've heard since he left home. My best friend, Lydia came taunting for days. 'Well, I hear your brother Jesus is calling himself the Messiah. Does this mean you will have a seat in his court when he comes into power?'"

Rebecca nodded. "Yes, and I thought Matthias would take

more than a passing interest in me until he found out my brother was Jesus, the religious fanatic."

Jude stepped closer to Mother. "Mother, could he be insane?"

"It was that time he stayed in the desert for forty days." Joseph said.

"You're right!" Simon said. "Too much sun!"

I felt a sharp tug on my arm and Mother was in the midst of us, turning slowly as she spoke to meet each of our gazes with her own. "Stop this! All of you. I will hear no more of this, do you understand?" She paused and stared at me. "How can you speak this way of your own brother?"

I glared back. "He is no longer our bother. He is now the Messiah." I spat. "We will speak with him and force him to go to Judea. If he is the Messiah, then let him reveal his power. Let him stand before the people and show them his strength and wisdom instead of wandering around the countryside preaching to the lost and destitute." I whirled and marched back down the shore. I didn't care if the others followed or not. I had to do this! The crowd parted as I made my way toward the door.

"Jesus, listen to me. It's about time you gave us some of your precious attention. Listen, you've been wandering around the countryside working miracles, so they say. Some say you've preached in the tabernacles. And, I heard that just a few weeks ago your preaching almost cost you your life in Judea."

Mother appeared beside me, breathing hard. "James! Stop it this instant. I will not listen to someone speak this way to a son of mine!"

I stiffened. "I am your son, too. Or have you forgotten the rest of us? I am tired of always taking second place to Jesus just because he thinks he is the Messiah." I turned and shouted toward the empty doorway into the house. The crowd parted around me, scurrying away like the little mice they were.

"If you are the Messiah, then go to Judea. Tomorrow, the Feast of the Tabernacle begins and there will be thousands at the temple. Go there and proclaim yourself Messiah in the temple. Show them your miracles. Stop this silly stalking around the countryside with fishermen and tax collectors." I turned to my brothers and sisters crowded around my disturbed Mother. "Leave Galilee and go to Judea, so that your disciples there may see the works you do. No one who wants to become a public figure acts in secret. Since you are doing these things, show yourself to the world."

The shadows inside the door diminished and my brother appeared. Sunlight illuminated his face. His eyes, filled with a quiet power, regarded me. I stared back defiantly. His gaze shifted to my brothers and sisters and settled on Mother. "My time is not yet here; for you any time will do." He looked back at me. "The world cannot hate you, but it hates me because I testify that its works are evil. You go to the festival. I am not going up to this festival, because my time has not yet fully come."

Anger boiled within me. "Your time has come and gone, Jesus. Don't fool these people anymore." I turned to the remaining crowd. "Hey, all of you, listen to me. I was there when Jesus was a teenager. I was there when he was sick. I was there when he fell and cut his head. I've seen him bleed. Can a Messiah bleed?"

Horrified faces pulled away from me. "He's just a man. Just a carpenter. Ask any of us. He's not the Messiah!"

I felt the strong grasp of my big brother on my arm. "James, it is time for us to go." Joseph said.

I jerked my arm out of his grasp. "I'm not finished! I've got more to say! I've kept my mouth shut for too long." I shoved my face into his. "Why don't you and Simon go swimming! Better yet, get one of his disciples to baptize you."

Mother stepped between us. "James! That is enough! Watch

your tongue. It is your most powerful weapon. Don't turn it on the ones who love you."

I stepped back from her. "I've stood in his shadow too long. And, I'm tired of it. If he is the Messiah, then let him prove himself. Perform a miracle. DO something. After all he did nothing when father was dying. Don't you remember?"

"Don't say these things, James. They are words you can never take back. Don't say them!" Mary said.

I shook my head. "Say what? That he stood by and let father die? That he stood there, his body filled with the power to heal and he did nothing?" I turned to the receding crowd. "Did you hear that? He did nothing? Just stood there with all the power of the universe at his disposal and he did nothing! What kind of Messiah is that?"

Jude took me by the arm. "Come on, James. Let's go."

Simon stepped into my vision, his youthful face red with embarrassment. "You've said enough, brother."

I pulled away from them, stumbling down to the shoreline. "No! He let father die. He let him die. Don't you understand?" Tears poured down my cheeks. I felt the cold water lap around my ankles. My brothers and sisters and my mother stood huddled before me. Behind them, illuminated by reflected light from the waves, Jesus looked out over the crowd. He didn't care about me. He didn't care about us. Only them! "He let Daddy die! Some Messiah!" I fell to my knees in the water and sobbed.

Jesus turned to go back into the house. I felt hands on my arms and I looked up into the tear streaked face of my mother. "James, his time had not yet come."

CHAPTER 4

THE DONKEY

*As they approached Jerusalem and came to Bethphage and Bethany at
the Mount of Olives, Jesus sent two of his disciples, saying to
them, "Go to the village ahead of you, and just as you enter it, you will
find a colt tied there, which no one has ever ridden. Untie it and bring
it here. If anyone asks you, 'Why are you doing this?' say, 'The Lord
needs it and will send it back here shortly.'"*
Mark 11:1-3 (NIV)

"My little child, the Lord needs your help."

Martha looked up from her breakfast and
squinted into the bright light. A man stood in the open doorway
to her house and the morning sun shone around him. She
couldn't see the man's face.

"Who are you?"

"A messenger of God, my child. Today, you will be asked to
help the Lord. When you are asked, will you help?"

Martha tried to pierce the bright light to see the man's face.
She stood up from the table and walked toward the light. "Of

course, I will help." She said. Suddenly, she tripped on something and fell forward. She tumbled to the ground and blinked.

Martha was surrounded by darkness and she sat up on the dirt floor of her house. The odor of the animals in the nearby stall wafted over her. She glanced toward the front door and saw only waning darkness as the dawn approached. She rubbed her eyes. It had only been a dream!

Something cold nuzzled her neck and she stood up to face the young foal of the family donkey. She ran her hands through the rough hair of the animal's face and looked into the deep, brown eyes.

"Nip, it was only a dream. Nothing is wrong."

Nip nuzzled Martha's chest with her nose and she reached to a nearby sack hanging just out of reach of Nip and her mother and retrieved some figs. She offered them to Nip and the colt nibbled them down.

"Who was the man, Nip? He said he was a messenger from God."

"A messenger from God?" A voice came from behind her. Martha turned to see her father step off the ladder leading up to the family bedroom. "Why are you down here in the manger? Your mat is up there with the rest of us."

Martha studied her father's tall, gangly figure and his long, black beard. "I wanted to sleep down here next to Nip. I'm going to miss her."

Her father squatted in front of her and ran his hand through Martha's hair. "You're only seven and you would not understand. Nip will bring us a healthy price that will feed us for three months! I told you when Nip was born that she would be sold one day."

Martha felt the tears well in her eyes and her chest grew heavy. She stepped back and embraced Nip's neck. "But Nip is part of our family."

Martha's father stood up and put his hands on his hips, his

long robe falling to the ground. He towered over Martha. "One day, you will have to make such decisions for what is best for your family. Nip will go on to live with a family who will love her as much as you do."

Martha looked into Nip's dark, brown eyes. Behind Nip, her mother moved into view and nudged her daughter with her nose. Nip pulled out of Martha's arms and moved back to feed from her mother.

Martha felt her father's hand on her shoulder. "Martha, there is a little girl out there who needs a Nip in her life. The scriptures tell us to be responsible for God's creations, including his animals. I will make sure whoever purchases Nip will take good care of her and love her as much as you do."

Martha nodded. "Father, I had a dream."

"You did?"

"A messenger from God told me the Lord would come to me today for help and I should help Him." Martha turned and looked into her father's eyes. "Is giving up Nip what the dream meant?"

Her father took the mother donkey's rope and opened the side door to their home. "Maybe so." He led the donkey and her colt out into the enclosed pin at the side of their home. "If we are faithful to Yahweh, He will bless us. But that means we may have to do something we do not understand. Stepping out and responding to Yahweh without question is the best kind of faith."

Martha's father tied the donkeys to a hitching post and squinted into the morning sun. "If the Lord asks you to help Him out today, then be sure and do that." Her father squatted in front of her. "But, be very careful of such a request. Make sure it is truly from God."

Martha nodded and picked up a bucket to fill the animal's drinking trough. "Yes, father."

"Now, start your chores. Food and water for the animals.

Then, go help your mother with the weaving." Her father disappeared into the house and Martha ran to the cistern and scooped up a bucket of water. She filled the water trough then put hay in the feeding trough. Nip nuzzled her again and she embraced the colt.

"I'm going to miss you, Nip. I don't want to let you go, but if you can bring love into the world, then I guess I'll have to learn to live with that." She wiped a tear from her eye. Martha carried the empty bucket back into the house. Voices rose outside and when she turned, two men had Nip and her mother by the rope and were untying them.

Martha ran out the door and slid to a halt. The two men glanced at her, and the look on their faces was not one of evil or deceit. Their faces were fair and open.

"What are you doing?" She said.

"The Lord has need of your animals." One of them said.

Martha blinked and a shadow fell over her as his father stepped into the enclosure. "May I help you?"

The second man nodded toward the donkey and the colt. "The Lord needs them and will send them back here shortly."

Martha put a hand out and stopped her father's forward advance. "Father, remember my dream? A messenger came to me. This is why."

Her father glared at the men and looked down at his daughter. "We can't just let them take away our animals, Martha!"

Martha glanced at her father's angry face and back at Nip. The animals were sedate, cooperative and this was very unusual for a donkey. She looked back at her father. "You said I should step out on faith. I believe these men. The Lord needs our animals and they will return them. Faith, father. Isn't that what you told me to have?"

Her father's face slackened and he crossed his arms. "I did say that."

Martha nodded and turned to the men. "If the Lord has need of our help, we are pleased to help Him."

The two men smiled and nodded and led the donkeys away. Nip cast one last look back at Martha and she felt her chest swell with joy mixed with sadness. Would she ever see Nip again? Would her faith be misplaced? Only the Lord knew.

CHAPTER 5

BY DARKNESS BOUND

A very large crowd spread their cloaks on the road, while others cut branches from the trees and spread them on the road. The crowds that went ahead of him and those that followed shouted, Hosanna to the Son of David!" "Blessed is he who comes in the name of the Lord!" "Hosanna in the highest heaven!" When Jesus entered Jerusalem, the whole city was stirred and asked, "Who is this?" The crowds answered, "This is Jesus, the prophet from Nazareth in Galilee."

Matthew 21:8-11 (NIV)

"*I*t is dark in here." The man's voice was shaky with fear. Good!

Saul pushed the tiny clay lamp across his wooden table toward the man. The shadows flickered and moved across the man's bearded face. "I prefer the darkness, Abner." He whispered.

Sweat ran from beneath the cloth on Abner's head and he licked his lips. "I followed the man like you asked me to."

Saul leaned into the flickering lamp light. "And, where did he go?"

"To the temple. He met with the High Council."

Saul nodded. "And, how was he received?"

"They laughed at him. I think he wants to betray his master. Force his hand." Abner ran a hand through his beard. "Why would he do such? This teacher is a good man."

Saul slammed his open palm on the table. "He is a blasphemer! A deceiver!"

"But, Saul, he has healed the sick. He has even raised Lazarus from the dead."

Saul stood up slowly and walked around the table. He leaned over the man and smelled the stale fish in his beard. "Do you support this enemy of our people? Do you follow his teachings?"

"Well, no."

"You are a coward, Abner. Take my money and leave me." Saul stood up and motioned toward the door as he dumped a few coins on the coarse wooden table.

Abner scooped up the coins and hid them in his robe. "Saul, the High Council is against this man, too. Why aren't you working with them?"

Saul opened the door allowing bright sunlight to gush into the room. He squinted into the rays of light. "The High Council sees this man as a charlatan. I see him as a usurper of the prophecies. They have no idea how heinous his crimes are. They do not appreciate my theories."

Abner stood up from his bench and moved into the sunlight. "Perhaps you have not yet decided about this man, Saul. Perhaps you wonder if his claims are true."

Saul shoved the man out into the sunlight. "Begone before I turn you into the High Council as a collaborator of this teacher."

Abner disappeared into the crowd milling in the streets. Saul had almost closed out the offending light when his ears detected the distant sounds of an unruly crowd.

Across the end of a distant alleyway, Saul watch as a procession of men and women scurried along, carrying palm fronds and flowers. As quickly as they appeared, they were gone followed by a most unusual sight. The man sat upon a donkey, riding in the midst of the surging crowd. The donkey's child, a colt tagged along behind. The man held his head high bearing the stature of a king. But his clothing betrayed the demeanor of a commoner.

Saul stepped out of the light into the shadows and reached for the door to close it. For a fleeting second, the man glanced in his direction. Their eyes met across the long alleyway. Panic welled in Saul and he caught his breath. The scant seconds stretched into an eternity and then, a blinding light reflected from some shiny surface in the surging crowd struck him in the eyes. He stumbled back away from the window temporarily blinded. He slammed the door and groped around the dark interior of his room until he found his table and chair. Darkness ruled the room once more. He sat carefully and waited in fear until his sight slowly returned.

"You think you are the Messiah? Well, I shall double my efforts at interpreting the Law. I shall seek out all heretics who blaspheme the name of Yahweh. Beware, man who would be God. Saul will not be so easily blinded by your deeds."

CHAPTER 6

BLINDED BY THE LIGHT

The man answered, "Now that is remarkable! You don't know where he comes from, yet he opened my eyes. We know that God does not listen to sinners. He listens to the godly person who does his will. Nobody has ever heard of opening the eyes of a man born blind. If this man were not from God, he could do nothing." To this they replied, "You were steeped in sin at birth; how dare you lecture us!" And they threw him out.

John 9:31-34 (NIV)

"Can you stand here before the High Court and expect us to believe you? Do not lie to Caiaphas, the high priest." Caiaphas spat the words at him.

Simeon was still amazed by the color red. He saw it now in the old priest's cheeks. They glowed with anger. Simeon resisted the urge to reach out his hands to touch those hot spots, to feel the heat he had never seen before this day.

"We don't believe you, boy!" The great, hulking figure backed away slowly, turning to survey a group of men dressed in black and white. Black and white. Black Simeon understood. That was all he had "seen" his entire life. White was new. It didn't seem to fit these men and their coarse, cruel words.

Simeon glanced at the pinched, drawn faces and back at Caiaphas. "I tell you this man healed my eyes. I was blind, but now I see."

The black robes seemed to swarm in on each other, milling in discontent and confusion. It made Simeon dizzy, for he was not used to seeing movement. He had only heard and felt.

Caiaphas' hand emerged from the ebon folds of his garment. "Bring in his parents."

Simeon watched his mother and father being escorted into the room. Tears welled in his eyes. He was *seeing* his mother! Simeon rushed across the room, his hands going instinctively to her face. The wrinkles looked just as they felt. Her chin was soft, her lips were full. Just as they had felt.

Simeon sensed his father behind him and he whirled to stare into his eyes. They were brown. How warm that color looked. Simeon's hands touched the bearded chin and felt the tears that streamed from his father's face.

"Is this your son?" Caiaphas spoke from behind him, his voice an unwelcome intrusion.

Simeon's mother and father looked at each other and then back at Simeon. "Yes!" His mother answered, joy in her heart.

"Do you know what he claims?"

"No." The father spoke.

"Tell them." Caiaphas gestured with his white hands.

Simeon swallowed nervously and rubbed moisture from his eyes. A small speck of clay fell into his open palm. "A man spat on the ground. And then he took clay made of the spittle and anointed my eyes. I remember feeling his face, so strong, so powerful. I felt his voice with my hands as he told me to go and wash in the pool of Siloam."

Simeon's voice began to crack with emotion. "Mother, when

I washed the clay away, I could see! And I turned to find this man who had healed me and he was gone! I never saw him. Oh, mother, the colors! The light!"

Simeon's mother clutched him to her chest, the tears flowing. "Oh, my son, you can see!"

"Then, this is your son who was blind from birth?"

"Yes. Why do you ask?" Simeon's father backed away from Caiaphas' imposing figure.

"This man," Caiaphas' voice shook with hatred as the dead white hand gestured at Simeon, "of whom your son speaks is not of Yahweh! He did not keep the sanctity of the Sabbath when he supposedly healed your son. He is a sinner! So how can a sinner who does not keep the Sabbath do such miracles?"

"This is our son. And, he was born blind." Simeon's father spoke quietly. Simeon looked away from his father and back to Caiaphas. The priest wore a grim expression.

"If any man confess that this Jesus is the Christ, he must be put out of the synagogue! What do you say?"

Simeon watched as his father's face darkened. His eyes grew hesitant. Simeon had never seen this before. He had only heard his father's voice filled with fear a few times in his lifetime. Now Simeon saw what it did to his father's countenance. "I only know that this is our son, and that he was born blind. But by what means he now sees, we do not know."

Simeon's mother's voice trembled with fear. This he had heard before. "We do not know who he speaks of."

"He is old enough to speak for himself." His father said. Simeon stared deep into his father's eyes at the confusion and doubt there. They were deep wells of emotion, pits of blackness that penetrated to the soul, a sight Simeon could not contend with. His father reached out his hands towards Simeon and turned him to face the assemblage of priests. Black and white and red. The colors were so vivid Simeon grew lightheaded.

What was his father saying? "He shall speak for himself." His father pushed him forward.

Simeon stood alone against the sea of faces. Faces he had only known by sound, never by such scowls and grimaces. Eyes that he had never been able to feel were windows into their souls, betraying the hatred, the anger, the condemnation that filled their voices.

"Whether this man, Jesus is a sinner or not, I cannot say." Simeon turned and searched his father's face. It was turned to the ground, the eyes averted. His mother wiped at her tears with her shawl. "All I know is that this morning I was blind and now I can see."

Caiaphas separated himself from the group and pushed his face into Simeon's. Simeon noticed the fine, red blood vessels that filled the whites of his eyes. He smelled the wine on his breath. He heard the scorn in the voice.

"We are Moses' disciples. You are his?"

Simeon backed away and turned to his parents. They looked at him helplessly. Simeon truly was on his own. He had to speak for himself.

"We know that God spoke to Moses." Caiaphas continued smugly. "As for this fellow, Jesus, we do not know where he comes from."

Simeon's heart raced and he turned to the rest of the priests. Could they not understand the miracle that stood before them? Could they not see? "Here before you stands a marvelous feat! You do not know where this man gets his power from and yet, he has opened my eyes! God does not hear sinners." Simeon felt his strength growing, his courage building. Yes, he could stand up for himself. All was so clear, now. He pointed to them all. "God only hears the righteous man. And, since the world began there has never been a man who opened the eyes of one born blind. Has there?"

The mass of black and white and red was silent. Simeon

turned to Caiaphas, fear no longer in his heart. Caiaphas was not as frightening as an eternity of darkness.

"If this man were not of God, he could do nothing." Simeon said.

Caiaphas backed away, his eyes wide in surprise. The chief priest glared at Simeon's parents and then back at Simeon. "You who were blind from birth were born in sin. And you dare to teach us? Begone! You are cast out of the synagogue!"

The words pierced Simeon's heart and he turned to his parents. They stood stricken; their eyes filled with fear. Simeon could not let this blemish fall on them. Pushing past his mother, he hurried out of the temple.

Outside, the sunlight that burned his face in the past, blinded him and for a moment he was back in his comfortable world. But he could not remain there. He had seen too much and he could never go back. Simeon had to find the Healer, Jesus. Simeon did not know what he looked like. He glanced down at his hands, the only eyes he had ever known. They would still serve him well for he knew the touch of the Teacher's face. He would find Him.

CHAPTER 7

THE COIN

"You still lack one thing. Sell all that you have and distribute to the
poor, and you will have treasure in heaven; and come, follow me."
    Luke 18:22 (NIV)

Sunlight scattered off the coins as Eli let the golden
disks cascade from one hand to the other. Normally,
the sensation brought him joy. But, since his encounter with
Jesus of Nazareth, his desire for the feel of the coins had
diminished.

"Give it all away?" He muttered, dropping all but one of the
coins in his tunic. "The man is insane! I can't give it all away!"

He shook his head as he walked along the rows of beggars
inside the temple, his eyes roving over the groveling figures. He
came to the spot closest to the Pool of Siloam. The bent and
deformed figure crouching in the dust was a stranger.

"Where is Simeon?"

The old woman looked up with a toothless mouth. "Who?"

"The blind boy? Where is he? I come here every week and give him a coin."

The old hag laughed wetly and wiped her lips. "Don't know. But you can give it to me."

Eli jerked his hand away as the old woman reached for the gold coin. He backed away until a hand rested on his shoulder.

"Eli, I see you still have your fortune."

Eli turned to see his friend Jabal surrounded by a group of Pharisees. "What do you mean?"

"We heard about your visit with the Teacher." Terah leaned forward, his lean, sharp nose reminded Eli of a vulture. Surrounding Terah were his fellow Herodians. Anger burned Eli's face. How dare someone loyal to the beast Herod question him. And yet, more and more, the Herodians had associated themselves with the Pharisees. Both wanted to see political independence for the Jewish people. Eli would prefer such "independence" not be under the rule of Herod.

"I don't know what you're talking about." Eli pulled away, walking down the rows of beggars toward the temple court-yard. Jabal appeared at his side, keeping pace with him.

"Oh, come now, Eli. We heard you went and asked the Teacher a great question. What was it, 'Master, are you the Messiah?'"

"That is not what I asked him."

Jabal stepped in front of Eli and halted his advance. The rest of the Pharisees hovered around him. "So, you did talk to him?"

"I heard you called him 'Good Teacher'." Terah smiled smugly.

"Very well. I did go and talk to him. And, yes, I did call him Good Teacher. He is a rabbi, after all. There is nothing wrong with that."

"Do you not know how he healed on the Sabbath?" Obed stepped forward, his bearded face hidden in shadow. "A blind boy. Right back there."

Eli tried to hide his surprise and glanced back toward the beggars. "Simeon?"

"He heals on the Sabbath. I hear he claims to be the Son of God." Terah spoke hoarsely.

Jabal winced. "Don't even hint of such blasphemy. Unless, of course, Eli here can assure us that this Jesus is not the Messiah. Just what did he tell you?"

"I didn't ask him if he was the Messiah. I asked him 'what shall I do to inherit eternal life?'. Don't tell me you have not wondered what lies beyond the grave? We speak of it often in our debates." Eli pushed passed them and stepped out into the open courtyard of the temple. Sunlight streamed down around him. Jabal appeared again at his side.

"And, is it true he told you to sell all that you have?"

Eli stopped, feeling the cold pressure of the coin in his hand. "Yes. He said it was not good enough just to keep the law. I had to sell all I had and distribute to the poor. And, then follow him."

Laughter burst around, raucous and derisive. Terah tapped the gold coin in Eli's hand. "The rich, young ruler sells all to follow a carpenter. How absurd. Doesn't he realize the poor are that way because they sin?"

Jabal did not laugh, rubbing his chin with his hand. "It disturbs me that you value the opinion of someone who thinks so poorly of the Law. Perhaps it is time we confronted him."

Terah pointed excitedly over their shoulders. "Here is your chance, Jabal. Witness the approach of the Teacher."

Eli whirled. Jesus and his disciples entered the temple courtyard, surrounded by a rabble of people. Jabal tugged at his tunic. "Come, Eli. Let us question your Good Teacher further."

Before Eli could stop him, Jabal was away, leading his crowd of vultures across the tiled floor of the temple. He watched as Jesus stopped, eyes fixed quietly on the approach of the Pharisees. Eli hesitantly followed, feeling the weight of the coin in his palm.

"Teacher," Jabal asked with just a touch of sarcasm in his voice, "We know that you are a man of integrity and that you teach the way of God in accordance with the truth. You aren't swayed by others, because you pay no attention to who they are. Tell us then, what is your opinion? Is it right to pay the imperial tax to Caesar or not?"

The crowd fell silent, all eyes turning to Jesus. Eli felt heat begin in the back of his neck and creep up into his hair. His face flushed as Jesus' eyes turned full onto him. Jesus' stare remained fixed; his eyes filled with a touch of incredible sadness. Jesus turned back to Jabal.

"Why do you test me, you hypocrites? Show me the tax money."

The gasp from the Pharisees was audible and sent a flock of doves scurrying into the sunlight. Jabal grinned wickedly and extended his hand toward Eli. "Eli, let me see your coin."

"What?" Eli gasped.

Jabal jerked his head toward Eli, his eyes filled with devious hatred. "The coin. Now! Surely a man of your wealth and position can spare one coin."

Eli hesitantly opened his hand, palm up and Jabal snatched the gold coin. Jabal handed the coin to Jesus.

Jesus delicately took the piece of gold, his eyes straying toward Eli. "Whose image and inscription is this?" He pointed to the face on the coin.

Jabal's face wrinkled in puzzlement. "Caesar's."

Jesus nodded and handed the coin back to Jabal. "Then render therefore to Caesar the things," He paused piercing Eli with his eyes, "that are Caesar's, and to God the things that are God's."

Jabal opened his mouth to speak, but no words came out. Jesus turned away and the moment of tension and silence broke in the rabble of the crowd. The people moved away as Jesus went his way, leaving Jabal and the Pharisees alone in the sunlight.

Terah spat on the ground and shook his head. "He is dead! I tell you; his time has come."

Eli reached for the coin. "Let's go, Jabal. You've tested the Teacher enough today. Now you know why his words trouble me so. Give me my coin."

Terah reached over Eli's shoulder and snatched the gold coin. "I have a better use for it. Perhaps I can convert it to silver. I know someone who can help us with this so-called Messiah."

Eli shook his head. "No! That coin is mine. Give it to me."

Terah laughed wickedly. "What's wrong with your devotion to our cause, Eli? Are you now going to follow this Jesus, even as he said you must do? Whose side are you on?"

Eli glanced at the coin gleaming in Terah's hand. "I don't really know anymore. Take the coin. Perhaps it will be put to good use." Shaking his head, he walked away sorrowful.

CHAPTER 8

THE UPPER ROOM

He replied, "Go into the city to a certain man and tell him, 'The Teacher says: My appointed time is near. I am going to celebrate the Passover with my disciples at your house.'" So the disciples did as Jesus had directed them and prepared the Passover.
Mark 14:18,19 (NIV)

I leaned on my walking stick and peeked around the corner into the alleyway. A dozen men huddled in the shadows deep in conversation. One man stepped from the crowd and motioned down the alleyway toward a nearby stairway. The men followed him up the stairs and disappeared through a doorway. I had been following them for the past hour through the busy streets of Jerusalem.

I glanced up at the noon day sun. "Barnabus, come here."

A man shuffled forward. He was young and wore a simple robe and head covering. "I need you to take care of the lamb for us."

"Yes, Josiah." Barnabus said quietly. "Your wife will be wondering where you are."

I sighed. "I know, Barnabus. I told her I was going to pick up the lamb from the temple. I need you to do that for me."

"It's Joseph, isn't it?" Barnabus glanced at the stairway.

"Barnabus, you have been a faithful servant to my family since your father passed away. Your father served me since the day we arrived in Jerusalem from Bethlehem. He was a faithful servant before you. I give you much liberty in being concerned about our affairs." I paused and smiled. I reached out and put a hand on the young man's shoulder. "You are like family to me. But you do not have a son. You do not know what it is like to have your own first born turn his back on his family."

"I am sorry, Josiah." Barnabus looked down. "I spoke out of turn."

"You spoke out of concern. Now, run along to the temple and get our lamb. Take it back to my wife and then you and the rest of the servants may go and spend Passover with your families."

Barnabus looked up abruptly and smiled. "Master, that is very kind of you. I will spend Passover with Rhoda's family. We are betrothed." He ran off and I shook my head. Barnabus was more of a son to me than my real son. I hobbled down the alleyway to the foot of the stairs and climbed them slowly. My age was catching up with me.

At the top of the stairs, I paused before the door. Just what was I doing? What was I to say to Joseph and his rabble? I had scarcely set foot inside the door into a small anteroom when a hand grabbed my arm and pulled me into the shadows. I glanced up into the face of an elderly woman.

"Who are you?"

"Josiah! Who are you?"

"The owner of this house. I was preparing the upper room

for the Master and his followers when these rebellious ruffians took over." She pointed to the room.

I pulled aside the curtains and looked into the chamber beyond. A low-lying table had been set with dishes for the evening Passover meal. Joseph, my son, and his friends sat around the table. One man stood at the head of the table holding a small bag.

"Will your plan work?" Joseph said. He sat at the side, his long, black hair filthy and matted with sweat and dust. He was far from ready to sit at the Passover meal! His feet were not even washed!

"It will work. Be ready to follow the Messiah when he is arrested. I must go or he will be suspicious." The short man with curly dark hair pocketed his bag in his robe and made his way toward me. I pulled back into the shadows. Who was this man? Was he the ringleader of this group? Had he led my son astray? I would end this nonsense! The woman pulled me back abruptly.

"No! I have sent for the guards. They are coming."

My heart seized and I grabbed my chest. "No! That is my son. They will take him away and throw him into prison."

The door burst open and harsh sunlight streamed in. A dozen of Herod's guards rushed into the room followed by a Roman centurion. The centurion, tall and muscular in his red and bronze armor motioned to the woman. "You are the one who sent for us?"

"Yes." She stepped forward. "They are plotting to overthrow the king."

Bedlam broke out in the room as the soldiers subdued the men and hustled them out the door.

"Sir, may I speak to that man? He is my son."

The centurion raised an eyebrow. "And, are you fomenting rebellion through your son?"

"No!" The woman said. "He came here hoping to stop him."

"Father?" Joseph shouted in the hands of two soldiers. The centurion motioned for them to pause.

"Son, I warned you." I said.

"Is this your doing? Have you betrayed me and your people?" My heart raced. "No! I came here to stop you, but I was too late."

The centurion leaned forward and glanced at Joseph's neck. He reached out and grabbed a golden necklace from Joseph's neck. He pulled it away and at the end of the necklace, a beautiful gem gleamed.

"Ah, here is Pilate's wife's necklace. Someone stole it and now we know why. To finance your rebellion."

"That was given to me by one of my friends." Joseph said.

"Which one?"

Joseph shook his head. The centurion held the gem up to Joseph's face. "You realize that a thief who is also a rebel has only one fate? Crucifixion!"

I fell backward into the arms of the older woman and she stumbled under my weight. "Please! No! My brother was crucified. Don't take my son."

The centurion motioned for the guards to take Joseph out of the room. He held up the gem. "I have no choice, old man. And, if you continue, then you will join your son on the cross." He whirled and left the room.

I stood there in the bright sunlight, my cheeks now stained with tears. "No! My son! Why!"

The elderly woman pushed me gently out the door. "I must get this room ready again for the Passover for the Master. You must go. I am sorry for you son, but he made his choice and now he must pay the consequences. But first I must get more water. They spilled all of my water. You can go get me some more water." She rested her hands on her hips.

"I am not your servant!" I protested. "My son was just arrested, and you want me to carry water?"

She leaned in close to me. "Your son was the one who upset the date cart. Your son and his friends ruined the room I was getting ready for the Master! The least you can do is fetch me some water. Besides, you will not be able to see your son right now. He will be taken to Herod's palace for determination of his fate. That will take a while. So, be off with you." She picked up a large urn and pushed it into my hands. "There is a well two streets over. Now, hurry!" She closed the door in my face.

I stood there fuming and almost threw the jar down the stairs. How dare that woman tell me what to do? I was a man, not some woman servant! I sat on the first step and realized I had left my walking stick in the woman's foyer. If I knocked on the door now and had no water to deliver, I would have to hear her protestations again. Besides, she was right. Joseph and his friends had created chaos and I was as responsible for the wrongdoings of my son as if I had done them myself. Painfully, I stood up and set out to find the well.

* * *

THE STREETS WERE GROWING MORE crowded as I hobbled along with the jar filled with water sitting on my shoulder. I dodged children running along and the occasional Roman soldier patrolling the streets.

"Always there is violence during Passover week." I growled. "And, my son had to be in the thick of it." I glanced behind me at the soldier I had just passed and noticed two men hurrying my way. Were they part of Joseph's army? Were they more rebels come to spy on me and report me to the centurion? I hurried as well as my painful hip would allow and finally made it to the house with the stairs. Gasping, I opened a door beneath the stairs and entered.

The elderly woman appeared from a hallway and the

fragrance of the elements of the Passover feast made my stomach growl. "You couldn't take the water up the stairs?"

I placed the water jar on a table and wiped sweat from my brow. "I am not much younger than you and carrying that jar of water through the bustling marketplace is not my idea of casual exertion."

She hissed and hefted the jar. "Men! You think your work is hard?" She disappeared into the depths of the house. I turned to leave and the door opened onto the street again revealing the two men.

"Here he is." One said.

I put up my hands in protest. "Just a moment. I had nothing to do with Joseph's crimes."

The other man's forehead furrowed in confusion. "You were carrying water along the street, weren't you?"

"Yes."

"This is not normally a man's job." The first man said. "The Master told us, 'Go into the city, and a man carrying a jar of water will meet you. Follow him. Say to the owner of the house he enters, "The Teacher asks: Where is my guest room, where I may eat the Passover with my disciples?" He will show you a large room upstairs, furnished and ready. Make preparations for us there.'"

I wiped more sweat from my brow. "The Master? The Master! I heard about the Master. Very well, follow me." I led them out into the street again and up the stairs. I opened the door and ushered them into the room beyond. The woman looked up from the table and for a moment, her face twisted in anger. But, when she saw the two men, she smiled. "Will you be needing my upper room tonight?"

"Yes. The Master said we would find a room upstairs, furnished and ready." The second man said.

The woman bowed her head. "I am honored and humbled that the Master and his disciples have chosen to eat in my room.

Yahweh told me in a dream to prepare this room and that a man carrying water would bring his disciples to me." She glanced once at me and smiled again.

I stepped back astonished and amazed. Was she telling the truth? If so, then Yahweh might also answer my prayers. I nodded once to the disciples of the Master and grabbing my walking stick, made my way down the stairs. What now? Joseph thought I had betrayed him! Could I stop his crucifixion? After the Passover feast, I would find my son. Yes, I would search for him wherever he was taken. No man could leave his son behind.

CHAPTER 9

THE BOWL

The evening meal was in progress, and the devil had already prompted Judas, the son of Simon Iscariot, to betray Jesus. Jesus knew that the Father had put all things under his power, and that he had come from God and was returning to God; so he got up from the meal, took off his outer clothing, and wrapped a towel around his waist. After that, he poured water into a basin and began to wash his disciples' feet, drying them with the towel that was wrapped around him.

John 13: 2-5 (NIV)

"There! It is finished!"

Reuben glanced up at his father as the man lifted the bowl from his table. His father blew away the final sawdust with his powerful lungs. His chest glistened with sweat and his mighty muscles rippled under the skin as he held the large bowl up to the fading afternoon sun. "Your mother will be able to prepare many meals in this bowl, my son." He smiled down at Reuben and for a moment, his happy features were marred by his obvious revulsion. Reuben could never become the man his father was.

"It's perfect, father." Unlike me, Reuben thought. He tried to straighten his crooked legs to get more height so he could see the bowl better, but pain shot through his legs. He moaned and his father placed the bowl on the worktable.

"I'll carry you back to the house as soon as I deliver this bowl, son."

Reuben collapsed back onto a stool. "I'm fine, father. I will just rest while you deliver the bowl."

His father's features clouded again with emotion as he turned and left the workroom. Reuben felt the familiar brush of shame. The priests had told them Reuben's weak legs were because of some past sin in his parents' life. His father and mother had both protested but to no avail. They were all unwelcome at the synagogue! Maybe the sin was his own! He was soon to be thirteen and no longer a child and yet his legs were no stronger. His thoughts were tumbling and wild as he felt the growing change into manhood. He was a sinner! He knew it! His father and mother's shame was HIS fault, not theirs.

What could he do? He pulled himself upright and took his walking sticks and hobbled across the work room. Behind a basket of rope, he had hidden his own project. Another bowl not as large as the one his father had made. But HE had carved it. HE had polished the exterior. And now, all that remained was to sand down the inside and the bowl would be complete.

He pulled the wooden bowl from its hiding place and managed to carry it over to his father's work bench. He placed the bowl on top of the sawdust and curls of carved wood from his mother's bowl. He leaned his walking sticks against the edge of the workbench and locked his legs in a stiff position.

He took the tools his father had left on the bench and began to grind away at the interior of the bowl. He placed oil on the wood and felt the fine grain respond to his actions. In the motion of this hands, he found solace. His arms and hands were normal, unlike his legs. He lifted the bowl and examined it in the fading sunlight. It was a bit lopsided. It was not perfect. But he had made it. By himself!

A shadow passed over the doorway to his father's workshop. A man stood silhouetted against the light outside. "Ananias?"

Reuben stiffened. "My father is not here."

The man stepped into the room. He was young and clad in a simple robe. He carried a sack filled with food. "I was looking for your father. I need a bowl to use in tonight's Passover feast and I heard he makes the best."

Reuben swallowed. "He just finished the only one left and took it home to my mother."

The man looked down at the workbench. "What of this one?"

Reuben raised an eyebrow in surprise. "It is not yet finished."

"How soon can you have it ready?"

Reuben felt a cool wave pass over his body. The man wanted HIS bowl? Even with its imperfections? "I am almost finished. Maybe an hour?"

The man nodded and glanced over his shoulder. "Very well. Can you bring it to the upper room?"

"Where?"

The man gave him instructions. Reuben felt his heart swell. The location was not that far. He could make it on his walking sticks. "I'll have it there within the hour. Long before sunset."

The man nodded and placed a coin on the workbench. "Good. The Master will be pleased." He turned and left the work room. Reuben picked up the coin and his eyes widened. He had gotten paid for his own work?

But then, he glanced up at the door in fear. What if his father returned before he finished? He wouldn't let him take the inferior workmanship of the bowl to the buyer. He would make him return the money.

Reuben studied the imperfect bowl. No. He would return the money and give them the bowl. He would admit to its warped nature and give the coin back to the man. But it would still be the bowl he had made. He picked up the sandstone and hurriedly polished the inside of the bowl. He had to finish before his father returned!

* * *

SWEAT POURED from Reuben's face as he crawled up the last step to the door leading into the upper room. The bowl was safely tucked into a sack over his shoulder. His walking sticks were tucked under his belt along his back. He collapsed on the hot stone and glanced over his shoulder at the sky. The sun was setting and he had barely made it in time. He knew his father would be searching for him so they could celebrate Passover together. But he had a bowl to deliver!

He pulled himself painfully to his feet and retrieved his walking sticks. He opened the door and hobbled into the welcoming cool of a foyer. The fragrance of food made his mouth water and his stomach growl. He heard voices in the distance and he made his way past benches laden with dishes and remnants of food. He was too late! The Passover feast was already underway! He leaned against the stone wall and took the bowl from his sack. He placed it on an empty table beside a pitcher of water. He placed the coin next to the bowl.

He was tired and sore and disappointed. No, *he* was a disappointment! He looked at the pitcher of water. His bowl was not good enough to serve food in! As he studied his lopsided creation, he realized it was good for only one thing! To wash dirty hands in.

Reuben heard voices again and lifted the curtain gently aside and peered into the upper room. The fragrance of roasted lamb and bitter herbs wafted over him. A low-lying set of wooden tables were arranged in a U shape. The disciples reclined around the table on cushions. They laughed. They smiled. They ate and drank. And in the center seat sat a man with his back to him. He was still and silent. What had the man said? The Master! Was this Jesus of Nazareth? Reuben had heard stories of the Master, the Teacher, the Healer and his disciples. Some people had been healed by this man. But surely it was because they were free from sin! Someone as sinful as Reuben could never hope for healing.

He sat down behind a table out of sight and fought to catch his breath. A curtain separated the room from the chamber beyond and the curtain moved aside. A man was silhouetted against the light for a moment and then the curtain fell back. The man moved passed the table behind which Reuben hid. His arm was illuminated by the small oil lamp he reached for on an upper shelf. The flickering light illuminated his face and he placed the lamp on the table with Reuben's bowl.

The man was swarthy with dark, curly hair and a heavy beard. His hands were thick and calloused, the hands of a worker. Just like the hands of his father! This had to be Jesus of Nazareth. He was also called the carpenter.

The man shrugged out of his robe and laid it across another table. His chest was exposed covered with dark, wiry hair. He wore only a loin cloth beneath the robe. He grabbed a heavy cloth from a shelf. He pulled the cloth back and unfurled it. The lamp light flickered in the wind from the cloth as the man wound it around his waist.

The man turned to the table and paused as he looked down at Reuben's bowl. He reached out a finger and touched the coin. For a moment, he was perfectly still and then he looked slowly over his shoulder in Reuben's direction. Reuben tried to shrink into the wall behind him. His face burned with shame as the man regarded the lopsided bowl.

Jesus blinked and nodded and ran his hand across the interior of the bowl. His fingers traced the edge of the bowl. He sighed and picked up the pitcher of water and poured water into the bowl. The plume of water fragmented the light from the lamp and cast prisms of rainbow colors across the wall above Reuben.

The man picked up a small wooden cup from the nearby table and plunged it into the water. He lifted the cup and droplets of water fell back into the bowl. He turned toward the curtain and Reuben could see the profile of his face. The man's lips moved with words Reuben could not hear. He opened his eyes and took a drink from the cup. He nodded in approval and placed the cup on the table before him. The water was not for washing! It was good water, drinkable water! And, Jesus of Nazareth had poured it into his bowl!

The man tossed the free end of the towel over a bare shoulder and placed his robe over his arm. He picked up the bowl of water. What was he going to do with the bowl? Jesus held the bowl at chest height and studied his reflection in the surface of the clear water. The man was acting like he was going to wash the feet of the others in the room! This was unthinkable! The tradition was for the lowest of servants to wash the feet of visitors to a house but not with the best water, certainly not with water clean enough to drink! But Jesus would use the best, the cleanest water to perform a menial task that was below even the lowest servant's responsibilities. How could a teacher, a rabbi, a masterful man of God do such a thing?

Jesus paused as he studied the surface of the water. His face was illuminated by shards of reflected light. Slowly he lifted his gaze and his eyes, clear and luminous, gleaming with the light of the cosmos turned in his direction. Reuben gasped and tried to push himself further into the wall behind him. That gaze! That look! Such power and mercy and forgiveness all wrapped into one prolonged glance! He felt his heart ache with the depth of his own sin, his own imperfections. How could this Jesus of Nazareth possibly even look at him?

The man turned and shouldered aside the curtain and returned to the upper room. Tears poured down Reuben' cheek. Why was he crying?

A voice softly whispered in her ear. "But whoever drinks from the water that I will give him will never get thirsty again. In fact, the water I will give him will become a well of water springing up in him for eternal life." He glanced about him. The antechamber was empty. Who had spoken? Reuben pushed painfully to his feet. He had to know what Jesus of Nazareth intended with his bowl and the water. He stumbled to the curtain and listened.

"Lord, are you going to wash my feet?" A man said gruffly.

"What I am doing you don't realize now, but afterward you will understand." A softer voice answered. The voice carried the power of eternity and an infinity of love.

"You will never wash my feet," the other man said.

Jesus replied, "If I don't wash you, you have no part with me."

A murmuring arose from the other men in the room. Then, in a voice filled with emotion and pain, the man who refused the washing said "Lord, not only my feet, but also my hands and my head."

This was too much! How could he stand here before such humility, such unconditional love, such mercy? He was worthless! Vile! Deformed! Cursed!

He leaned back into the shadows. It would be best if he ceased to exist in the face of such humility. The curtain was thrown aside as a man hurried past the Reuben and paused at the door. He turned and looked back at the upper room and for an instant, light and shadows played across his coarse features. His eyes were wide in shock and sweat beaded on his forehead. His breath came quick and shallow. He glanced once at the coin on the table. He snapped it up and tucked it into a pouch. Then, he opened the doorway onto the bleak darkness of night and hurried down the stairs. Cool air wafted through the open doorway. The breeze stirred the oil lamp flames.

Reuben did not understand what was happening. This man was one of the Master's followers, surely. And yet, he had left the company of his master. What was the man up to?

He retrieved his walking sticks and started toward the door. It was past time for the Passover feast. His father would be looking for him. He would confess his unworthiness. Perhaps it would be best if he were cast out of his family to spare them any guilt and remorse.

He paused beside the table where once his bowl had stood. The Master had chosen his bowl to wash his disciples' feet. His marred, imperfect bowl. Just like him, warped and twisted. And yet, the Master had chosen the bowl. He had used it to wash feet with clean, drinkable water. Something divine had happened here and Reuben had been privileged to witness it.

He looked at the small wooden cup of water. The Master's lips had touched this cup. They had touched this water. The Master had looked at him and then there had been that voice in his head. Could it be? Was he worthy?

He lifted the cup. "Yahweh, I am not worthy but will you cleanse me even now? Will you wash away my iniquity? Will you make my robes as white as snow?" He lifted the cup to his lips and drank.

The water was cold and sweet; not with the taste of honey; but with the sweetness of the purest water in the universe. He held it in his mouth and let it trickle back along his tongue. It reached the back of his parched throat and the coolness began to spread into his neck and down his spine. The cold liquid shot down through his chest and into his abdomen.

The water was no longer cold. It was a burning, scorching fire that scoured his insides and still he stifled his screams. The fire exploded from his middle and coursed outward along his spine, down his legs. The heat cooled to a warm wave that slowly made its way down to his toes. His legs felt heavy and he glanced down.

They were no longer thin and wasted! They were full and tense with muscle! He placed the cup on the table and stood up on strong, but shaky legs. He shoved his hands over his mouth to stifle the laughter of joy, but the tears poured down his cheeks.

He walked to the door and pulled it open and stood at the top of the stairs. He RAN down the stairs and into the courtyard, laughing and spinning in a dance he had never been capable of.

This night, the Master's love and humility had healed him. His sins were forgiven in the wave of love and unconditional forgiveness the Master represented. He paused and glanced once more at the open door to the upper room. He had left his bowl and his walking sticks. He no longer needed them. It was time to run home and find his father and mother and tell them the Good News! He sprinted down the narrow road toward his home beneath a sky filled with stars. He was healed and his world would never be the same again!

CHAPTER 10

THE ROPE

When Judas, who had betrayed him, saw that Jesus was condemned,
he was seized with remorse and returned the thirty pieces of silver to
the chief priests and the elders. "I have sinned," he said, "for I have
betrayed innocent blood." "What is that to us?" they replied. "That's
your responsibility." So Judas threw the money into the temple and
left. Then he went away and hanged himself.
Matthew 27:3-5 (NIV)

*A*aron looked up from counting his money as the two
men entered his shop. They were dressed in simple
robes, their faces covered with black cloth, only their eyes visible. He quickly rolled the denarii he had been counting into a
small piece of cloth and tucked it into the merchandise laying
before him on his table.

The men had not come to the shop to purchase anything.
They ignored the baskets, the ropes, the various artifacts that
hung from nails around his small shop and walked straight
across the floor to the table.

"It's time to pay up, Aaron." One of the men said as he slammed his fist down on the table. Various bits of merchandise clattered together from the sudden violence of the man's blow. Aaron leaned back on his stool, his heart picking up its pace. He was having trouble breathing. He was getting too old for this nonsense.

"You tell your master that I will pay him when I have the money. I know that I own him a great deal, but I can only pay so much at a time."

The second man picked up a small basket from the table and held it in the air in front of him. "Perhaps a few years in debtor's prison will change your mind, Aaron."

"What good will it do for your master to throw me in debtor's prison? If I am not selling my goods, how can I ever repay him?"

"What goods?" The second man said as he dropped the basket on the floor. He turned with his arms outstretched as if to look around the room and Aaron heard the unmistakable crunch as his foot descended on the basket. The first man leaned across the table. His hand deftly snaked in among the merchandise and snared the small pouch.

"We'll consider this a down payment. Next time that may not be a basket that gets crunched. It may be your head."

The two men whirled and left the room. Aaron stood shakily, his body trembling with fear. He had trouble catching his breath and his hand came to his chest. He heard a sound behind him. Ruth appeared through the folds of the doorway leading from the shop to the small room beyond, the extent of their home.

"Aaron, what was all that racket?"

Aaron leaned against the table to catch his breath and his wife instantly was at his side. Her hands touched his shoulder, patted his back.

"More of Seth's henchmen come to aggravate me about the debt that we owe. Ruth, what are we going to do?"

Ruth pressed a hand to her lips. Aaron turned to look at her and saw tears in the corners of her eyes. "Oh Aaron, will we have to sell the shop?"

"Never! I will never sell this shop and give in to the likes of Seth and his money hungry hoard. I'll go to debtor's prison before I let him take this away from us."

Ruth shook her head. "If you go to debtor's prison, I will go with you. I will not stay here alone to run this shop."

"Ruth, your love is so strong. I don't know what I would have done without you all these years. I'm afraid it's hopeless. They took our last denarii. There is no way we can make enough money to pay Seth."

Ruth reached up and touched his lips with her hand and shook her head gently. "Never say there is no hope, Aaron. There is always hope. God will provide for us."

Aaron shook his head and pushed her hand away from his lips. "God will provide. Just where was God when these two men were threatening to crush my head like a basket?"

Ruth opened her mouth to answer but was interrupted by a sound at the door. A man stepped into the room and brought with him all of the darkness that was outside. He glanced around at the room cautiously, his eyes gleaming in the bright light from the lamps. Aaron swallowed hard and glanced at his wife.

"I'm afraid sir that we are about to close up shop for the evening."

The man's eyes appeared wild and animal-like. He darted around the room, searching for something.

"Sir, I said that we were closing." Aaron stated once more as he pushed Ruth behind him.

The man stepped forward to the table. "No! You cannot close. You must help me."

The ferocity of his voice startled Aaron and he leaned back away from the man's wild eyes. Was he another one of Seth's men come to harass him? Behind him he felt Ruth pat him in the middle of the back and he turned to glance at her face. Her skin was white, her face pale with fear and she shook her head gently. He placed a finger to his lips and motioned to the back door. Reluctantly, she left him and disappeared through the curtains.

"Very well." Aaron stated as he turned around. "Just what is it that you search for?"

"Rope." The man stated, his eyes roving around the room.

"Rope?" Aaron asked him.

"Yes. And not just any rope will do. It has to be a certain type of rope."

Aaron stepped around the table and motioned to the wall to his left. "I have several types of rope here. I have braided myself. There are ropes that are small enough for a tiny animal and ropes that are big enough for an ox."

The man leaned towards Aaron and his eyes fixed on the wall beyond. Several loops of rope hung on wooden pegs.

"You say that you have braided these yourself?"

"Yes." Aaron stated proudly. "It's one of my better products. I'm very proud of my work. My father taught me how to braid ropes when I was a small child. You will find that my ropes are some of the best in town. Is that why you came here? Because of my fine reputation?"

The man glanced at Aaron as if he were crazy. "No. I don't know why I chose your shop. I just need a rope."

The man reached over to a nearby loop of rope and took it from the wooden peg. He felt the caliber of the rope, stretched it out from hand to hand and jerked on it.

"How strong is this one?"

"It's medium strength." Aaron stated as he reached and took

the rope from the man. "It could probably corral and guide a small donkey."

"That won't we strong enough." The man stated loudly. His eyes were even more wild now. His face was covered with a thin sheen of sweat. "I need something strong enough to hold up the weight of a man."

Silence came into the room. Aaron could smell the sweat of the man, his fear. He gently took the rope in the man's hands, coiled it and hung it back on its wooden peg. Immediately beneath that peg was another loop of rope. He handed it to the man.

"This one will hold up your weight."

The man looked at the rope and gave it a few test tugs. He nodded briskly. "Good. How much?"

Aaron looked at the rope and rubbed his lip. "Let me think."

"I don't have time for any bargaining. Here, take this." The man interrupted him. He tossed a leather bag on the front of the table. Aaron glanced down at the bag and tentatively picked it up. He loosened the leather strap and opened the top to look in. His eyes grew wide in amazement.

"These are pieces of silver."

The man eyed him wildly and shook his head. "No. You are too kind. You don't deserve that money." His hand snaked out quickly to snare the bag from Aaron's hands. He closed the bag and tucked it into the sash of his robe and then searched the other side of his sash. He brought out a coin and placed it on the table.

"This should be enough. I think you deserve it far more than you do those thirty pieces of silver."

Aaron studied the meager coin. It was enough to cover the rope. But he needed far more money to satisfy Seth's thugs. He picked up the coin and it burned in his hand and he dropped it into a small basket to the side of the table. He glanced at his hand where red scorch marks rose in his skin.

"What is this?" He held up his hand.

"I'm sorry. I found that coin on a table in the upper room. Is it enough for the rope?"

"Yes." Aaron said and rubbed his hands together as the burning sensation went away.

The man hefted the rope over his shoulder and started for the door. He stopped and glanced over his shoulder at Aaron. "It was touched by the Master. That is why I could not keep it." He disappeared into the night.

Ruth appeared through the doorway. "Aaron, what is going on?"

"I don't know Ruth. That man just gave me enough money for a small piece of rope." He pointed to the basket.

Ruth glanced at the basket and her eyes grew wide. "How much did you tell him the rope cost?"

"I didn't. He gave me a coin. And, it burned my hand."

Ruth lifted the small basket and shook it. The sound of coins rattling against one another filled the silence. Aaron grabbed the basket and poured the contents on the table. Dozens of coins piled onto the wood.

"What? How? There was only one coin!"

Ruth smiled. "See. God does answer prayers. This will be enough to pay off our debt!"

Aaron blinked in shock. "But, how?" He picked up one of the coins and smiled. "He said the coin had been touched by the Master!"

* * *

AARON HAD trouble sleeping that night. He finally arose before dawn and sat on his roof watching the sun rise. What had happened to the man who purchased the rope? And, he had said the coin had been touched by the Master. Aaron had been on the mountain side when the Teacher preached a moving and powerful sermon. His followers had called the Teacher, Master. Was this man one of Jesus' followers? He stood up and started down his ladder. He had to find the man. If he had harmed himself with the rope, then Aaron was to blame.

The cool of the morning would soon be burned away by the rising sun. Where should he start to find the man. He spied a neighbor shopkeeper opening his stall.

"Ben, did you see a man leave my shop last night?"

Ben yawned and rubbed his eyes. "Aaron, I must confess that my wife made me sleep outside last night. Too much wine. I did see a man leave your shop and make his way to the ravine."

Aaron nodded and hurried down the street filled with dying shadows. He reached the ravine and heard the birds before he saw the body.

There, dangling from a tree something dark moved in the wind. He stepped hesitantly from the alleyway into the opening along the hillside. A tree stood there, its branches reaching towards heaven. It was a barren tree. It was a dead tree. Hanging from the lower limbs was the man who had bought the rope. His body swayed in the breeze, stiffening in death.

Aaron glanced at the ground beneath his feet and the brown pouch that had held the silver coins lay on the dirt. It was collapsed. Empty. He knelt and started to reach for the pouch until he remembered the man's words. He did not understand what had transpired. For some reason the silver coins in the pouch represented something far more evil than he could ever imagine.

There was a shuffling in the alleyway behind him and he turned to see two Pharisees standing at the edge of the alleyway. They glanced at him for a moment and then looked beyond him to the figure hanging from the tree. One leaned to the other and they whispered among themselves.

"Is he dead?" One of the Pharisees spoke to him.

Aaron stood and glanced down at the ground. "Yes. Why do you care? Who was this man?"

"The pouch. Could you pick it up for us and make sure there are no coins left inside?" The other man said.

Aaron grimaced. What were these men playing at? "You can pick up the pouch yourself. It is evil."

The first Pharisee nodded. "That is why we cannot use the coins or touch the pouch. They are tainted by this man's sin."

"What shall we do with the coins, then?" The second Pharisee asked.

"It is against the law to put this into the treasury, since it is blood money." The first man said.

"Use it for the man's funeral." Aaron said.

Both men glared at him. "He is a sinner. There is no place to bury him." The second man pointed to the hanging man.

"Then take the money and put it toward something good." Aaron said.

The first man massaged his beard. "We do need a place for foreigners, for sinners who have forsaken Yahweh. Perhaps we can use the money to buy that potter's field as a burial place for foreigners."

"Yes!" The second man said. "A Field of Blood for the forsaken."

"Is that supposed to buy you penance with God?" Aaron said. "You make me ill. This man was in pain and has ended his life and all you can talk about is burying him like you want to bury your own sins."

The Pharisees straightened and glared at him. "What synagogue to you attend?" The first man said.

Aaron spat on the ground. "That is none of your business." He stormed past the men as the morning sun cast a long shadow of the tree and the dead man across the Pharisees faces. He stopped outside his doorway and looked up at his name carved into the doorpost. Yes, God had answered his prayer. That he now truly believed. He would pay off the debt to Seth and he would keep his shop. Shaking his head, he muttered a prayer of thanks and stepped into the house to greet his waiting wife.

NOTE: There are many who think Judas did not die until after the resurrection. The discussion of this is beyond this simple story. Whenever Judas chose to end his life, the remorse and guilt that prompted it did not change. I ask the reader to study this event if they are interested in learning when Judas died. The point is, he died at his own hands.

CHAPTER 11

THE ROOSTER

"Truly I tell you," Jesus answered, "this very night, before the rooster crows, you will disown me three times."
   Matthew 26:34 (NIV)

"**W**here do you think you're going?"

Silas paused at the doorway and turned to look sheepishly at his mother.

"Out. I'm just going out with some friends."

His mother wiped her hands on a rough cloth and pushed her shawl away from her forehead.

"First, you're going to tell me what this is." She pulled something out of her robe and dangled it in his face. It was a long, red cloth with a small conical scrap of leather tied to the end.

Silas squirmed and reached out to take the string from her hand. "Just something I've been playing with. With the other guys, you know."

"Uh huh." She didn't seem to be convinced. "Looks like it might fit over a bird's beak."

"A bird?" His voice broke.

"You better not be taking that rooster with you."

Silas winced inwardly and tried to smile. "Mother, you already told me I had to stop cock fighting. I'm just going out with some of my friends."

His mother looked at him skeptically and planted her hands on her hips. "Oh, how I wish your father was still alive. I don't know if I'll ever get you raised. Promise me you won't go to those fights anymore. Promise me."

Silas swallowed. "I promise, mother. I promise."

She turned away, shaking her head. "Don't stay out too late."

Silas slipped through the door and out into the night. He paused to glance back through the closing door at his mother. She seemed so tired, so lonely. He hated what he was about to do. But tonight, was the most important fight of the year. He slipped around the edge of the house to the back. The rooster strutted in his small pin with the three hens. His red comb shook as he walked across the pin to meet his master. Silas grabbed him quickly, slipping the muzzle over his beak before he could make a sound. Sliding the struggling, feathered body under his arm, he made one last glance at his house and then slipped down the alleyway.

"I'm sorry, mother. I can't keep my promise tonight."

* * *

THE BATTLE WAS NEARING its culmination. Silas cheered loudly as his rooster delivered the final blow and the other cock slumped to the bloody sand. Silas bounded into the battle ring in triumph and scooped up his rooster in excitement. The other boys and their combatants seemed less enthusiastic and slowly dispersed leaving Silas to his victory. He watched his friends slowly walk away and felt his feelings of victory crumble.

"It's just as well." He rubbed the feathers of his rooster. "We are the victors. They're just jealous." He glanced up between the walls that enclosed the alley at the stars gleaming in the cool night air. He wondered what time it was.

"It is after midnight." He heard an all too familiar voice behind him. He whirled.

"Mother? What are you doing here?"

She stepped out of the shadows, her face hidden by the veil and heavy cloak that draped her figure.

"You lied to me, Silas. You promised."

Without warning the rooster let forth a loud crow, echoing eerily through the silent streets. Silas soothed his troubled bird.

"This is the last fight, mother. The very last. I couldn't miss it."

She pulled back the veil from her face and her eyes burned with emotion. "Silas, a vow is not to be taken lightly. A promise is given with trust from a heart of love. You have crushed my heart beneath your feet."

The rooster struggled beneath his arm as if feeling the guilt that surged in Silas' own heart. Suddenly it let forth with another raucous crow. The sound pierced to Silas' soul, a lonely, accusing sound. He shivered in the cool air.

"Mother, I am truly sorry. I don't know what to say."

She nodded and lifted an eyebrow as if she were going to smile. She didn't. "I am going to do something that you least expect, Silas."

He backed away from her gaze until he felt the hard, pebbly surface of the alley wall behind him. What punishment was she going to wreak on him now? Whatever it was, he realized he deserved it.

"I am going to do something far worse than to punish you." She paused before him, her features suddenly melting, her eyes becoming moist. "You see, I love you, Silas. And you realize now the pain you have caused. Therefore, I am going to forgive you."

The rooster burst from under his arm, striking the ground in a dead run. It hurtled away into the dark alley letting forth a blood-curdling crow. Silas gazed after the receding bird and looked back at his mother.

Her face was once again hidden by the veil and she turned quietly, disappearing into the darkness. He was torn between her receding figure and the desire to find the rooster. Silas ran into the darkened alleyway and found the rooster perched sedately on a broken column. He gingerly took the bird under his arm.

"I think it is time we go home. For good." Footsteps echoed at the end of the alleyway and a figure eclipsed the starlight from the open courtyard. A man ran toward him and stopped just inside the cone of light thrown against the alley wall by a torch. His features were wild, his eyes wide in fear and amazement.

"Did your rooster crow?" He gasped, struggling for breath.

Silas backed away fearfully. "Yes. I hope it did not awaken you."

The man's face paled and tears formed at the corners of his eyes, running down his cheeks into his beard. He began to shake his head, his hands reaching up to knead through his wild, unkempt hair.

"No." He whispered and pushed past Silas down the alleyway.

Silas stood there puzzled in the flickering torchlight and listened to the man's sobs echo from the darkness. He glanced down at his rooster and walked into the darkness.

"Sir? Sir?" He whispered as he neared the end of the alleyway.

The sobbing lessened and the man's face arose from his slumped figure, his tear-filled eyes catching the flickering torch light. "What do you want of me?"

71

"If I did something wrong, I'm sorry. I can't seem to do anything right tonight."

The man gazed at him for a long period and then shook his head, his eyes falling to the dusty ground. "No. You have done nothing wrong. It is I who have failed."

"Failed? What happened?"

The man wiped at his nose and sat forward into the light. His hands were huge, calloused. "I betrayed my Master. I made a promise and I broke it."

Silas' heart leaped in his chest and he felt the familiar burning of guilt. He recalled the image of his mother's eyes changing from anger to love.

"Surely, it wasn't that bad. I did the same thing tonight. I broke a promise to my mother." He ruffled the feathers of the rooster. "I know how you feel. It hurts."

The man shook his head. "There is no way you can know how I feel. My broken promise goes beyond what you did. I have betrayed the person I love the most."

Silas knelt beside the man. "Sir, I don't know what to say that would make you feel better. But, my mother did something very strange. I thought she was going to punish me. You know, hate me for the rest of my life. But you know what she did?"

"What?"

"She forgave me. If this person really cares for you as much as you do for them, then they will forgive you, too."

The man's face softened, his eyes shifting back and forth as he studied Silas' face. His lips thinned and he almost smiled. "Do you think? He could forgive me for what I have done?"

The man stood up shakily. "He has forgiven so many. I once asked him, 'Lord, how many times shall I forgive my brother or sister who sins against me? Up to seven times?' And he said, 'I tell you, not seven times, but seventy-seven times.' Maybe that is what this is all about." He looked at Silas and he seemed to grow six inches, his features hardening in determination. "Maybe He is going to forgive us all. That is all I can hope for."

He stepped away into the darkness. Silas smiled and rubbed his rooster's feathers. "Seems like you taught me a lesson tonight. Let's go home. I have something to tell mother. I want her to know I love her."

CHAPTER 12

THE CELL

The true light that gives light to everyone was coming into the world.
He was in the world, and though the world was made through
him, the world did not recognize him. He came to that which was his
own, but his own did not receive him.
    John 1:9-11 (NIV)

The banging on the outer door echoed through the
house. I sat up slowly in my bed and glanced at my
sleeping wife beside me. Not that I had slept much after cele-
brating a dour Passover knowing my son was in Pilate's prison.

Who could be at the door in the early hours of the morning?
My heart raced with anxiety and fear. Already, Jerusalem was a
tinderbox waiting to explode with rebellious fire! Factions
moved and jostled in the shadows plotting the downfall of the
Romans. It had always been so at Passover time.

My hip ached as I stood up and more knocking echoed
through the house. I hurried from my bedroom and down the
corridor to the living area. The remnants of our Passover meal

still sat at the table. Rachel had been in too much pain to clean the tables and I had sent our servants to their quarters earlier so they could observe Passover with their own families. There was no one to clean up our mess or attend to a knocking at the door. My sleeping robe billowed around me as I unlatched the heavy, wooden double doors and peeked out.

"Father! Let me in!"

"Sybil?" I said. I pulled the heavy doors open and my daughter slid into the foyer. "What are you doing out after dark? Does Moab know you are out in the dangerous streets of Jerusalem?"

Sybil wore a dark cloak over her robe and her head was covered with a black cowl. "No, father. It is still the Passover. Everyone is at home."

"As you should be!" I kept my voice down and glanced back toward my bedroom. "We don't want to wake your mother."

Sybil wiped at her eyes and grabbed my hands. "If anyone would have stopped me, I would have told them I am the daughter of Josiah, the builder. Your fame and fortune alone would protect me."

"Unless someone would want to hold you for ransom!"

"Father, it is Joseph." She said urgently and descended into sobs.

I straightened and pulled my hands from hers. "Do you mean Didymus or whatever it is he calls himself now?"

Sybil paused and gasped. "I don't care what he calls himself. He is my brother." She put her hands to her face and stifled her sobs. "Oh, father, he will always be your son and my brother. And, he has been arrested. He is in Herod's palace in the holding cells." Sybil lurched forward and grabbed my arms, falling to her knees. "Please, father. You have influence. You have wealth. You must do something or tomorrow, he will be crucified."

I could not tell her of my encounter with Joseph in the upper room or that I already knew he had been arrested. I sighed and helped her to her feet. "Daughter, your brother left this family behind a year ago when he joined the rebels. He has too much of his uncle in him. I never should have named him after my brother."

"What are you doing here, Sybil?"

I whirled. Rachel stood in the doorway from our bedroom. "My dear, go back to bed." I said.

Sybil ran to her mother and in hushed tones told her what had happened. My wife looked over our daughter's shoulder and her eyes filled with fire. "Of course, your father will do whatever it takes. He knows some of the guards in Herod's palace. He will pay Joseph a visit tonight." She raised an eyebrow. "Won't you, dear?"

"Sybil. Rachel. I must tell you that I witnessed Joseph's arrest this evening. I tried to stop his arrest then, but the guards wouldn't hear of it." I rubbed my forehead and shook my head. "I am afraid Joseph is lost to us. He no longer identifies with our family."

Rachel gently pushed Sybil aside and closed the distance between us far more quickly than I ever thought was possible. Her eyes burned with fire. "I don't care what Joseph said. He is our son. You will do what you can to get him released. Then, together, we can talk some sense into him."

My heart lurched in resignation. "Yes, I will get my clothes on." It would be no use arguing with her and Sybil. The two had ganged up on me years ago when my wife told Sybil how I had torn them away from our home in Bethlehem. No matter that Herod had indeed had all male infants two years of age and under slaughtered. No matter that our son would have perished in the slaughter. Herod had managed to hush up the tragedy and even now, only thirty-one years later, the memory of that heinous crime by the current king Herod had been forgotten. No one wanted to challenge Herod's claim to be a benevolent king interceding for the Jewish nation with the Romans. Oddly enough, the only ally had been my son. I never should have told him about the slaughter. It only fueled his hatred of the Roman's and their puppet king.

* * *

I FOUND ZOPHAR, one of the guards at Herod's palace, a scant hour later. We stood beneath gleaming stars in a black sky as I dropped the coins in his hand. He nodded and escorted me through the back hallways of the palace to a dank and slime covered set of stairs leading down into the dungeon. Another guard stood at the stairs and Zophar spoke quietly to him.

At first, the guard glared at me until I held up a coin. His features softened and he held out his hand. "If Caiaphas' men show up, I never saw you." He hissed. I nodded and made my way carefully down the stairs. Zophar led the way before me holding up a torch. The air was cold and humid and filled with the vilest odor I had ever encountered. Body odor and decay and death and body excretions from years of prisoners waiting their turn on the cross. This prison was not for incarceration. It was merely a holding area for the crucifixions. Only dead men were kept here.

Zophar paused at the base of the stairs and handed me the torch. "Down that way. There are four prisoners in holding tonight. You can't miss them. You have less than an hour before they are brought up just before dawn."

I nodded and Zophar disappeared back up the stairs into the darkness of Herod's palace. I gagged at the smells and carefully made my way across the slippery stone floor. Words had been carved into the walls all cursing the Romans. Areas of scratched out words testified to Herod's attempt to erase any complaints about his rule.

I heard the voices before I got to the cells. Two voices raised in anger and fury. Without the torch, the chamber was completely dark. And yet, in the face of certain death and in a place of such foul stench and evil darkness, the two men argued. I came abreast with their cells. Two stone chambers with iron gates. Two men stood at the gates trying their best to face each other as they screamed and shouted obscenities.

I did not recognize the first man. He squinted in the light of my torch. "Who are you? Come to taunt us more?"

"I am Josiah, father of Joseph." I said.

The other man gasped. I turned to my son, his arms hanging through the bars of his cell door. His hair was long and matted and his face covered with dirt and clotted blood. "You! Traitor!" He said. "You followed us tonight to our meeting place and then called the guards on us."

"Joseph, I did not betray you. I came to find you to talk some sense into you before you went too far. I failed you."

His eyes filled with tears and then he stiffened and wiped them angrily from his face. "There is no one named Joseph here. Joseph died a year ago when he was disowned by his family."

I swallowed. "I am not sorry for that, Joseph."

"Stop calling me that!"

"I warned you what would happen if you continued to fight with these rebels."

He laughed. "You, with your growing business and your wealth and status with the Herod lovers! You, living in the best part of Jerusalem. You and your Greek ways!" He spat and the warm spittle hit me in the face.

"Son, you are to be crucified!"

"We know that." The other man said. "I tried to warn him. Rebelling is one thing but stealing in the name of the rebellion is punishable by death."

"They would not listen to me." Another voice came from a far cell. I walked toward the distant cell and paused at the sound of mumbled prayer. I paused before the cell next to Joseph's and before the cell of the man who had spoken. Against the back wall, a man knelt in prayer. His face was covered with bruises and his white robe was stained with blood.

"He's the Messiah." I heard the new voice to my left.

I studied the older, heavily muscled man in the next cell. "Who are you?"

"Barabbas, they call me. So, you are Joseph's father?"

"My name is no longer Joseph!" My son screamed from his cell.

"Yes, and I have enough coins to bribe the guards to release him. Perhaps to release you all." I said.

"No!" Joseph said. "I will gladly die for my cause. The oppression of my people must end. He did nothing about it."

"He?"

"The one who claims to be the Messiah." Barabbas said nodding to the cell with the praying man. "We all expected him to rise up when he was arrested. We were ready to follow him in insurgency. But this entire Passover week has been far from liberating. He rode into Jerusalem as a king, but he will be taken down from his cross a broken and defeated man. Just another false Messiah." Barabbas turned and moved to the back of his cell. "And, there is no amount of money that will buy my freedom. The Romans have sought me far too long."

I nodded. "Then, they will not care if one of your lesser rebels is missing from his cell."

"Not one." The first prisoner said down the hall. "Two. Take us both. If your son wants to stay and die, then take me!" Joseph let loose another string of obscenities and the two began to argue again.

I started toward my son's cell and something tickled at the back of my head. I paused and turned back to the third cell. The praying man was standing now with his back to me. Slowly, he turned, and I looked into deeply haunting eyes. He studied me for so long and suddenly I saw a vision. A star gleamed in the night sky. Gold. Frankincense. Myrrh. A young boy holding sheep carved from wood. An empty chair sitting outside my door. I dropped the torch and it went out. Complete darkness engulfed us, and my son started screaming and shouting for the guards.

I stumbled back away from the man's cell until the sharp rocks on the far wall of the corridor cut into my back. How could this be? Was this the young boy? Was this Joseph and Mary's son? But the angels had announced he would be king! The magi came from the East to bring him gifts. Gold for a king! Frankincense for an intercessory priest! I felt tears in my eyes as my thoughts on the last gift washed over me. Myrrh, the herb of death. What had the white clad Magi said that night? The king would suffer and sacrifice himself for his kingdom as Isaiah had predicted? I had to admit it had been years since I had considered the scriptures. I slumped to the ground as my son stopped screaming and silence filled the underground chamber. Then, slowly, the quiet susurration of the man from Bethlehem's prayers once again fell softly upon my ears.

Zophar appeared on the stairs with a torch. "Josiah! You must go now. They are coming for one of the prisoners."

I stood up slowly and in the flickering torch light paused once more before my son's cell. He stood defiantly at the back of the cell. "Joseph, remember what I told you about the young boy in Bethlehem? Remember what I told you the Magi said? He would be a servant king, not a conquering king?"

Joseph blinked. "What?"

I pointed to the cell next to me as Zophar arrived with his torch. He picked up my extinguished torch and lit it from his. Both flames filled Joseph's cell with flickering light. Joseph came toward me. "I don't care what your prophecies said, old man." He hissed at me. "If he is the Messiah, then bring down the angelic army! Slay the oppressors! Unless he does that, I would never honor him as a king!" Joseph turned his back to me and retreated into the shadows. I felt Zophar's hand on my arm.

"We must go now!"

I cast one last look at the man from Bethlehem as he knelt in his chamber and listened to his quiet prayers. All around me were nothing but lost causes. Where was Yahweh now? I followed Zophar up the stairs into the growing dawn of a day of death.

CHAPTER 13

DEATH SPICE

When they saw the star, they were overjoyed. On coming to the house, they saw the child with his mother Mary, and they bowed down and worshiped him. Then they opened their treasures and presented him with gifts of gold, frankincense and myrrh.

Matthew 2:10-11 (NIV)

"*A*nd, as you can see, one hundred pounds of myrrh." Zedekiah held out his hand. "We agreed on the cost before I delivered."

The older man in a gray robe sighed. "We agreed you were charging twice what most myrrh dealers charge." He held out a leather pouch. "Here is what I agreed on."

Zedekiah snatched the pouch from the man's hands and poured the coins into his own palm. He quickly counted the coins. "Very well. You drive a hard bargain."

"I am answerable to the Sanhedrin. They don't throw their coins away." The older man pointed to a doorway leading beneath Solomon's Colonnade into the rooms along the outer rim of the temple. "You may put the myrrh in there."

Zedekiah poured the coins back into his pouch. "Whose burial is this myrrh to be saved for?"

"Not that it is any of your concern. But, if you must know, Joseph of Arimethea has authorized the purchase of this myrrh. Now, unload your containers in that room and leave the temple area."

Zekekiah looked around. People were conspicuously absent from the frenzied activity that surrounded the temple at Passover. "Where is everyone?"

"There are crucifixions today. The criminals must be off their crosses before sunset." The elder priest said.

"So, it takes all of the priests to supervise a crucifixion?"

The man raised an eyebrow and growled. "No. But, there is one criminal in particular we want to make sure gets his punishment."

"A thief?" Zedekiah patted the pouch. "Like you, perhaps?"

The priest's cheeks reddened. "If you think you have been robbed, my good friend, then return the coins and be off with your myrrh."

"Where else would you find it? I am the number one dealer of myrrh in Jerusalem." Zedekiah pocketed the pouch. Truth was, it was more than double what the priest should have paid. "Never mind. I take back my comments. You have been only fair."

I led my donkey laden with the bags of myrrh along the outer rim of the temple. Animals were not traditionally allowed in the temple unless they were for a sacrifice. But I had the priest's permission. I offloaded the bags in the room he had indicated leaving only the baskets on the donkey's back that still contained limbs of the myrrh tree. I would give them to my wife. The small limbs would give off a pleasant fragrance for a couple of weeks and then we would remove the thorns before throwing the limbs into the fire for more aromatic heavenly scents. My wife used the thorns for sewing.

I was almost to the outer gates of the city when two Roman soldiers confronted me. "Where are you going?" One of them said in his worst approximation of my own language.

"I am Zedekiah, the myrrh dealer. I have delivered my load for the day and I am headed out of the city to my home."

One of the Roman soldiers chuckled. "Myrrh? I hear it works miracles." He leaned over the basket and plunged in his hand before I could stop him. His screams of pain made my donkey lurch and I held fast to his rope.

"Careful! The myrrh limbs have very strong thorns."

The Roman solider cursed in Latin and glared at me. "I could have you thrown in prison for that."

My heart raced and I bowed my head. "Forgive me for not warning you. Myrrh is the resin taken from the tree trunk. I placed small holes in the trunk and the resin leaks out and hardens. That is what I harvest. But, the branches of the tree carry very long thorns. My wife uses them for sewing."

The Roman soldier sucked on his finger. "Sewing, huh?" He stepped up to me and pulled out his sword. He placed the tip under my chin and slowly lifted my head to where I could make eye contact. "I wonder if they are strong enough to drive through your hands into the wood of a cross?"

I swallowed. "I do not think so. The worst they can do is cause great pain to the individual." I fumbled in my pocket and removed the pouch. "Perhaps I can make restitution for your pain?"

The Roman soldier's eyes lit up at the sight of the pouch. He snatched it from my grasp and shook it by his ear. "I think you just made a great deal. Your coins for your life."

The other Roman soldier stood quietly with his arms crossed. "Are you finished with this little fish? We have a king to kill."

I watched the pouch disappear into the folds of the soldier's tunic. "King?" I said.

The second soldier glared at me. "Your king. Claims he is your Messiah. But then there have been others. So far, none of them have come down off their cross."

The first soldier looked at the blood dripping from his punctured finger and then he glanced at the thorn limbs in the basket. He took the pouch out of his tunic and tossed it to me. "For your animal and your thorns."

I caught the pouch. "What?"

"We have a king to crown and a steed for him to ride on,"

"You fool!" The second soldier said. "He is to be flogged. He'll never ride a donkey."

The first soldier took the limbs of the myrrh tree from the basket and gingerly began to weave them into a circle. "Well, then a crown of thorns will have to be the only part of his coronation."

The Roman soldiers laughed raucously and marched away. I gripped the pouch of coins and looked at my donkey. "Thank you, Yahweh for paying my ransom." I slid the pouch into my pocket. "A crown of thorns for a supposed king. So, this is why the priests were so upset." I leaned over and looked my donkey in the eye, "And, I pray that this time, he is the real Messiah!"

CHAPTER 14

THE ROBE — PART 1

Then the governor's soldiers took Jesus into the Praetorium and gathered the whole company of soldiers around him. They stripped him and put a scarlet robe on him, and then twisted together a crown of thorns and set it on his head. They put a staff in his right hand. Then they knelt in front of him and mocked him. "Hail, king of the Jews!" they said. They spit on him, and took the staff and struck him on the head again and again.
Matthew 27:27-30 (NIV)

*J*onathan stepped into the dim interior of his home. Compared to the mid-day sun outside it was pitch black. He had a hard time seeing his mother across the room. She sat huddled in the corner, her back turned toward him.

"Mother, are you all right?" His voice carried across the room.

His mother turned suddenly, glancing at him with a fearful

look. She let forth a long sigh and stood to walk across the room to him.

"Oh, Jonathan, I thought you were your father. I was so frightened that he would find me."

Jonathan reached out and took her shaking shoulders in his hand. "Mother, do not be afraid. Father will not be home for a long while today. What is it that you are doing that you're so afraid father will discover?"

Jonathan noticed that his mother held something behind her back. She glanced over her shoulder and then brought forth the material that was clutched in her hands. "Let's move into the sunlight from the window so that you can see it."

His mother held the sheet of material before her into the slanting rays of sunlight coming from a window in the corner of the small room. In the light, the material shown a deep livid crimson. Its color was rich and vibrant. Jonathan reached forth a trembling hand and touched the soft material.

"Mother, it's beautiful. What is it?"

"It is a robe that I have woven for you, son. I began it the day that you were born and now that you are approaching the day of your passage into manhood, it will be my gift for you on this Passover."

Jonathan clutched the soft robe in his hands. "Mother, you shouldn't have. It's beautiful. Look, there are no seams in it." Jonathan glanced up and noticed tears in his mother's eyes.

"Yes, that is why it took so long. It is one seamless cloth."

A loud rustle came from the door to the room and sudden ripe sunlight gushed into the interior. The sunlight streaming into the door froze Jonathan into his tracks, the robe held out in front of him. His mother glanced to her left and grabbed the robe and pulled it out of his grasp. There, silhouetted in the bright sunlight stood the figure of a man. He stumbled into the room and slammed the door shut behind him onto darkness.

"Zillah, I'm home. Give me some wine."

Jonathan glanced up at his father as he stumbled across the room.

"What are you looking at Jonathan? Why aren't you out there working in the shop, trying to make some decent craft so we can make a little money in this home?"

Jonathan stood his ground, his face impassive and steeled against the anger of his father. He studied the man's face, lined with worry and the wrinkles from years spent in the sun. The man's eyes were red and his breath reeked of wine. "What good would it do for me to make any money, father? You would only gamble it away."

Jonathan watched the man's eyes light with anger and before he could stop it, the man's hand came up against the side of his face in a blow that sent his teeth rattling. He tasted blood in his mouth.

"Don't talk to me that way, boy." Jonathan's father roared. "What's happened to your respect for me?"

Jonathan wiped at his lips and noticed blood on his fingertips. "You have to earn respect father. You can't demand it."

Jonathan's father glanced over to his right, towards Zillah, standing in the corner of the room. "What are you hiding behind your back, woman?"

Zillah trembled and her eyes moved to meet those of Jonathan. "Oh, Nathan, please don't do this."

Nathan pushed his son roughly aside and whirled the woman around in the darkness. The robe fell onto the dusty floor of the room. It lay there nestled in the square of sunlight coming through the window.

"Well, what have we here?" Nathan stammered as he bent over and lifted the robe from the floor. "So, this is what you've been spending your hours on in the evening. Instead of taking care of me and cooking my meals, you've been weaving this cloth for our son."

Jonathan watched as his mother pulled vainly at the cloth

and Nathan jerked it out of her grasp. "Oh, Nathan, please don't tear it. I've spent my life making it for our son. Don't you understand?"

Nathan glanced down at the robe and then up at his son. "The only thing that I understand is how much money this will bring. I'm going to the market and see how much money I can get out of it."

Zillah fell to her knees, her voice rising in a wail as she grasped Nathan's leg. "No, Nathan. Don't gamble this away, too. You've gambled our whole life away. You've gambled our savings away. You can't give this away. It is filled with the love that I have for my son. Can't you see that?"

Nathan glanced down at her and pushed her roughly away and she fell backwards into the dust in the floor. He started towards the door and Jonathan barred his way, throwing his body against the door.

"Father, the robe is mine. You have no right to it."

Nathan's eyes met Jonathan's gaze and with a sudden spurt of violence, he grabbed his son by the throat and shoved him roughly aside. The door opened once again allowing the bright sunshine to enter the room. "Everything in this house belongs to me. Do you understand?"

Jonathan watched as his father stumbled out into the bright sunlight and he rose to his feet to follow him. The air was filled with heat and dust as if the particles were stirred by the feet of many animals. His father hurried away down the alleyway. Jonathan followed him. His father made his way down the street, which was now beginning to fill with a large mob of people.

Many times in the past, Jonathan had followed him before to find out just exactly what he did during the day. He knew where his father was headed. The Roman soldiers favored gambling, especially with the pitiful Jews. He was hoping he could get money from them and not at the marketplace.

Jonathan made his way through the gathering crowd and he saw his father slip down an alleyway by the side of Herod's palace and through an open archway in a stone fence. He followed, pushing his way through the crowd until he came to the doorway. A Roman soldier stood there at attention and his sword and his spear barred the way. Jonathan stood in the archway and watched the open courtyard beyond.

"Your kind are not allowed in here." The soldier growled. Jonathan fell back. It was true. Any good Jewish man would never set foot on the pagan soil where Pontius Pilate has established his throne. He craned his neck to look over the short wall in front of him. Something very strange was happening. There in the shadows of the courtyard stood Pontius Pilate himself. Beside him stood a Roman centurion. To his right was a group of soldiers, laughing, slapping each other on the back and Jonathan spied his father sitting in the dust nearby. The robe was clutched to his chest and there was a greed and lust in his father's eyes that he had seen before.

In the center of the court was another man. He was bent over a wooden post. He had been stripped of his clothing exposing his bare back and buttocks. A Roman soldier arose from a table covered with all types of implements. He shrugged out of his armor and wore only a thin tunic. He removed his helmet and his arms muscles and chest stretched the thin fabric.

The soldier spoke in his native tongue to the men around him and they laughed. He picked up a whip. The long, leather handle gave way to multiple strands of leather. Tied into the strands of leather were bits of bone and coarse glass and metal. The soldier hefted the cat of nine tails and brought it above his head, slamming the strands into the tabletop. Wooden chips flew and the men around him laughed even more.

Jonathan swallowed and watched as Pilate walked away from the shadows back towards his courtyard. The soldier turned his attention to the man tied to the post. The cat of nine tails swung through the air and the bits of metal and bone and glass seated themselves into the man's back.

The man arched in pain and the soldier jerked the cat of nine tails backwards, dragging the imbedded bits into the man's flesh and then flaying it away. Blood showered into the soldier's face. He laughed and wiped away the blood.

Jonathan collapsed against the wall, averting his eyes from the man at the post. He grew sick and nauseated and listened as more lashes fell. And yet, throughout it all, the man never cried out. He never screamed.

Jonathan had heard that flogging was used to make the criminal confess his crime. Why didn't the man cry out? Why didn't he confess? He could stop this any moment. Could it be the man was innocent? Only an innocent man would not confess, for only an innocent man would have committed no crime. The lashes ceased and more voices raised this time calling for the soldier to stop.

Jonathan knew that the men who were flogged were called the walking dead. The goal was to bring them to the brink of death. If a soldier killed a man in flogging, he himself could be flogged. The torture was finely tuned and well executed by the "lictor" as they were called. Why did Yahweh allow this to happen to His people? He stood up shakily and leaned against the wall.

The man on the post fell to the side into a puddle of his own blood and flayed flesh. His back was covered with lashes. The flesh was torn and blood and shreds of skin hung from the open wounds. The centurion who stood center court was wrapping the cat-o-nine tails back into a mass and he tossed it to his right, towards the corner.

The centurion turned to his soldiers and motioned and they began to laugh as they neared the figure in the center of the courtyard. One of them untied the man's hands and pulled him roughly up from the wooden post. The man turned, his face filled with agony. Jonathan looked deeply into his eyes and saw there a power and compassion he could not even begin to understand. For a moment their eyes met. Jonathan felt a jolt of shame and guilt as if he was the reason this man was suffering. Why? Who was he? The teacher? The healer? He had seen him once in the temple courtyard when he had overturned the money changers' tables. This was the man who many said had healed and preached and taught love and forgiveness. Is this why he was being killed? He turned to the soldier beside him.

"Why are they doing this to this man? He doesn't deserve to be treated that way. He's the teacher."

The soldier ignored him and behind the soldier, Nathan stood slowly to his feet and stumbled across the courtyard. His face was no longer slack in drunkenness. What they had just witnessed had sobered his father! Nathan's gaze met Jonathan's and his eyes were filled with a deepening horror.

"Father let's go." Jonathan beckoned to him. "You don't want them to turn against us."

Nathan's face remained a mask of strange expression. No longer was there anger, no longer was there scorn there. He looked at his son and there were tears in his eyes. "Is this how I've treated you and your mother? Is this what it has come down to that my love has turned to such cruelty?"

"Yes, father. But we still love you. We know that the demon of gambling has ruled your soul. Come home with us now."

A shadow eclipsed them and Jonathan looked up into the face of the Roman centurion. "Well, Nathan. What have you come to gamble for today?"

Nathan glanced up at the centurion and then back at his son."Nothing. We were just leaving."

He laughed deeply and pushed the man roughly back against the stone wall. Jonathan reached out towards his father and the man pushed him aside roughly also.

"Be careful, Judean. Your father owes us a debt.He lost just this morning, casting lots. I hope you've brought payment. If not, we can tie you up on the post where your king was just flogged and use you for practice."

Nathan was silent, his mouth open in fear and he glanced over at Jonathan. "I have nothing to pay you sir.I can't gamble anymore. It's destroying my life; it's destroying my family."

The centurion laughed out loud. "Are you having a sudden attack of conscience? Listen here, you little weasel. Once a gambler, always a gambler. There is nothing that could save your retched little soul. What is that you have in your hands?"

Jonathan's eyes fell to the robe even as his father's did.He watched as his father wadded the robe into a small bundle and pressed it behind his back. "Just a piece of cloth. It's really nothing. Please let us go."

The centurion reached behind the Nathan's back and jerked the robe from his grasp. He held it up into the bright sunlight. "Why, it looks like a robe. A royal robe. How fitting that we should now find a royal robe with which to coronate the king. Listen, little man. Take your son and get out of here and don't return. Consider this robe a payment on your debt."

The centurion turned abruptly and Jonathan watched as his father's hands snaked after the robe. Jonathan reached out and grabbed his father's arm.

"Father, let it go. It's certainly payment enough for us to have our father back."

Nathan watched as the soldier draped the scarlet cloth over the Teacher's bloody shoulders. The man turned, his eyes filled with tears and pain and for a second, Jonathan watched as his father's eyes locked with those of the man.

"That robe has bought my redemption, son. I swear that I will get it back for you. Go home to your mother. Tell her what you've seen here. I will follow this man and these Roman soldiers and with God as my witness, I shall retrieve your robe of manhood."

CHAPTER 15

THE BASIN

When Pilate saw that he was getting nowhere, but that instead an uproar was starting, he took water and washed his hands in front of the crowd. "I am innocent of this man's blood," he said. "It is your responsibility!"
Matthew 27:24 (NIV)

*M*iriam awoke from a restless sleep to the voice of her mother calling. She quickly arose from the small pallet in the corner of the one-roomed hovel that she called home. Across the dim room she saw her mother's figure huddled in the far corner on her own pallet. Early morning sunlight streamed through the slats of the wooden window and one pale beam cast its rays across her mother's hair.

Miriam hurried across the room and knelt beside her mother. Her mother lay on her side, her face turned away from the center of the room. Miriam reached out to touch her face.

"Mother, you're hot." Her tiny voice echoed in the room. Her mother lay back and Miriam saw the beads of sweat that covered her face. She saw the stains where the sweat had soaked through the armpits.

"Miriam." Her mother's voice was weak. "I am ill. It is the fever. You must go and work for us today."

Miriam shook her tiny head and pressed her hands to her lips. "Mother, I can't. I can't work without you. Besides, who will take care of you? Should I go get the healer?"

Miriam's mother shook her head and her eyes moved back into the ray of sunshine coming through the window. "My dear daughter, I will survive. Do not be concerned about me. Do be concerned about our job. If you do not show up today to represent us, we may die in debtor's prison."

Miriam stood shakily, her heart pounding in fear. She was only eleven years old. What her mother asked was impossible. There was no way she could do the job that both of them had done for the last year while they had tried to stay out of debtor's prison.

"Mother, I shall go and summon the healer and then I shall go and work for us today." Her voice sounded very tiny and the fear in her was very great. But as she stood there and watched her mother lying on the pallet, she knew that she had no choice. This was the legacy that her father had left them both. At his death he had left her mother strapped with an incredible debt from which they were only now recovering. He had left Miriam with a robbed childhood, forced to mature far quicker than she would have ordinarily done.

Miriam filled a pitcher with water and sat it before her mother along with some unleavened bread and dried figs. Then she hurried from the room, and down the dusty streets, to the home of the healer.

After the healer agreed to go and check on her mother, she set off toward the distant palace where she was to work for her mother today. As always, the immensity of Herod's palace awed her. Its great arching rooflines and immense rooms swallowed her and made her feel as small as a camel's flea. She hurried through the back entrance of the palace and passed the guards who allowed her to pass without any question. She reached the slave quarters and prepared for her daily duties. Roma awaited her.

"Well, you little wench, just where have you been? You're over an hour late for your daily duties. And where is that sorry excuse of a mother of yours?"

Miriam drew a deep breath and felt her heart once again pound within her chest and it threatened to explode through her skin. She shook and she trembled as she swallowed back the fear. "Mistress Roma, you must forgive me for being late. My mother is quite ill this morning and I had to attend to her needs."

"Your mother is ill?" Roma's voice dripped with disdain. "And just who will tend to your duties today?"

Miriam stood a little taller and looked the woman straight in the eyes. "I will."

Roma's laughter echoed through the darkness of the slave quarters. "We shall see, little flea." Roma chuckled. "You had best rinse yourself off in one of the baths and then get dressed. You're fortunate today. Pilate is late for his morning audience due to some very troublesome political matters that came up during the night. He hasn't missed you. Yet. But I suggest that you hurry. And remember this one thing." Roma bent over until her beady eyes rested only a few inches from Miriam's nose. "I'll be watching you. One slip up and it's off to debtor's prison for you and your mother."

Roma stood stiffly in her white tunic and turned and left the room. Miriam fought back tears and her lip quivered as she threatened to cry. She looked heavenward, her eyes peering toward the ceiling.

"Heavenly Father, please help Mom feel better today and help me with this job."

She hurried into the depths of the slave quarters where a small bath filled with tepid water stood. She stripped and cleansed her body until her skin shown with a nice pink color. She towel-dried her hair and then slipped on the golden and white raiment that her and her mother wore as servants of Pilate.

When her mother had taken on the job in the slave quarters, she had marveled at the beauty of the clothing. She had gazed at the golden thread interwoven through the white fabric with envy and anticipation. Whenever she donned the outfit, she felt very important, very aristocratic, very Roman.

But as the days passed, she watched the endless parade of pilgrims begging for the mercy of the Roman state. All of them had been denied and Pilate's anger and wrath knew no end. A day had come when she no longer wanted to wear the clothing of the Roman slaves. But until the debt was paid, they had no choice.

Miriam heard the clapping of hands and knew that Roma was waiting her. She hurried through the hanging golden beadwork that led into Pilate's audience room. Roma stood severely near the back of the room and motioned to her with a crooked finger. The room was empty and near the center of the room, sat a small golden throne. Miriam hurried across the room and stood stiffly next to Roma.

"Now you had better be on your best behavior today little girl. If you mess up one time, just remember what kind of lingering death awaits you and your mother in debtor's prison."

Miriam tried not to look up at the woman and her piercing black eyes and crooked nose. Roma suddenly stiffened and Miriam's eyes came to rest on the far doorway as Pontius Pilate entered the room. Pilate wore a white robe and a bronze breastplate. His thinning hair was carefully combed. But his face was far from pleasant.

He was followed by two Roman soldiers, one of whom was

most likely a Roman centurion. Both of them were arguing among themselves and Pontius Pilate had the world-weary look upon his face that she had seen settle in during the months she had worked for him. Pilate collapsed in the golden throne with a sigh and a look of exasperation. He snapped the fingers of his right hand three times.

Miriam bolted into action and hurried across to a small, low table near the wall. She retrieved a golden pitcher filled with wine and a goblet. She brought the goblet and the pitcher across the room and placed the goblet in Pontius Pilate's outstretched hand.

Carefully, she lifted the heavy golden pitcher and poured wine into the goblet, proud of the fact that she was not wavering. However, at the last second her strength seemed to give, and a small trickle of wine spilled over the edge of the goblet onto Pilate's hand. Only then did Pilate glance over at her, a look of utter hatred and disgust in his face.

"Be careful, you little wretch. Just what do you think you're doing? Wait. You're the little girl. Where is your mother?"

Miriam cast her eyes downward to the floor as she had learned to do.

"My mother could not work today. I am taking her place."

Pilate exchanged the goblet from his right hand to his left and shook the right hand until the fine droplets of wine splattered onto Miriam's face.

"Well, don't just stand there like a dolt. Go and get me a towel and my basin."

Miriam turned and hurried through the golden beaded doorway into the darkness of the slave quarters. She retrieved a white cloth lined with gold thread from a nearby table. In the far corner sat Pilate's basin. When she had first seen it, it had filled her mind with images of faraway lands and exotic places. She dreamed of one day being a princess sitting upon a throne with the fruit filled basin nestled in her lap.

The basin itself was as wide as her shoulders and made from gleaming polished gold. Around its upper edge were jewel upon jewel; rubies, sapphires, emeralds. Even in the dimness of the slave quarters the jewels winked at her with bright glistening light. She lifted the heavy basin and stumbled slightly under the weight. Hurrying through the doorway she went once again to the table at the side of the room. She took another clay pitcher filled with water and poured in into the basin.

Pontius Pilate was arguing heatedly with the Roman centurion and the soldier when Miriam arrived. She held the basin out and without looking, Pontius dipped his right hand into it and rinsed the wine from his skin.

Miriam backed away and sat the basin on a table behind Pilate's throne. Taking the white cloth, she carefully dried the man's skin. She took the towel, draped it on her arm, and stepped away into the shadows behind the throne. Miriam had done a good job, but she did not expect any words of thanks. The mere fact that she would escape any notice was reward enough.

Pilate suddenly stood from his throne and motioned to the outer doorway and Miriam began to focus on the words that were passing between he and the Roman centurion. They were rapidly speaking Latin, a language that she did not even begin to understand. However, her months spent in Pilate's palace had acquainted her with some of the more familiar phrases. Pilate was instructing the Roman soldiers to bring someone before him.

A figure suddenly eclipsed the brightness of the doorway leading into Pilate's room. The Roman soldiers marched across to the doorway and motioned for the figure to come into the room. Miriam had a hard time seeing the man's face backlit by the bright sunlight. She could tell that he was almost nude, wearing only a loincloth. Something bristling and wooden wrapped itself around his forehead. As he stepped closer, she began to see the blood that streaked his shoulders. Blood streamed from the crown of thorns around his forehead. Blood ran down his arms and dripped onto the ground. A beautifully woven robe of crimson draped over his torn shoulders.

Miriam winced, her hands coming to her lips and she glanced over at Roma standing in the shadows. For an odd moment, Roma's face seemed to soften. There within the lined features of that harsh caricature of a woman, Miriam saw a flicker of compassion.

"So, you say that you are the King of the Jews?" Miriam heard Pontius speak almost flawlessly in her native tongue.

The man stood there quietly, hands at his side, blood dripping down his face. His eyes were filled with bright fire. Miriam could not tell if it was the pain he felt or if it was utter madness. He stood silently before Pilate, as Pilate circled him once, twice; his eyes never leaving the man's face.

"I asked you a question. Are you the King of the Jews?"

The man studied Pilate's face and then glanced once in her direction. When their eyes met, Miriam felt a shiver travel over her body. This man did not deserve this kind of treatment. The look in his eyes changed from a fiery defiant glare to a soft, concerned expression. Suddenly she felt a wave of love and compassion and more importantly, understanding. This man understood her! He knew what she was going through! How? And, how could Pilate treat him that way? She had to grit her teeth to keep from crying out. The man looked back at Pilate.

"Is that your own idea," he asked, "or did others talk to you about me?" His voice was strong and powerful in spite of his injuries.

"Am I a Jew?" Pilate replied. "Like this pitiful child? Your own people and chief priests handed you over to me. What is it you have done?"

Miriam studied the man's blood streaked face. His gaze rested on her for a moment and she felt reassurance. His gaze shifted back to Pilate. "My kingdom is not of this world. If it were, my servants would fight to prevent my arrest by the Jewish leaders. But now my kingdom is from another place."

"Aha! You are a king, then!" Pilate said.

The man grew very still. Miriam felt the air thicken as if a storm brewed on the horizon. The hair on her skin bristled and she felt cold all over. Power entered the man's voice as he said, "You say that I am a king. In fact, the reason I was born and came into the world is to testify to the truth. Everyone on the side of truth listens to me."

Pilate froze and placed his hands on his hips. He turned and his gaze swept around the room, flickering over her like she was an insignificant rat in the corner. He whirled and shook a finger in the man's face. "Then answer me this one question. What is truth?"

Pilate laughed and clapped his hands. "We shall let your own people decide what is to be done with you. That will be the truth!"

Pilate motioned to the Roman soldiers. They shoved the man across the room, through the bright shaft of sunlight and out onto Pilate's porch. Pilate motioned to Miriam and she tore her eyes away from the receding figure. She followed Pilate as he strode out onto the porch where she stood in the shadows.

The courtyard in front of Pilate's palace was filled with a mob of people unlike any she had ever seen. Faces bobbed and weaved in a chaotic ocean of humanity. Pilate stood quietly at the edge of the porch, the man to his right. The crowd fell silent and Pilate paused as he regarded them.

"This man has done no evil that I can discern. He is an innocent man. What would you have that I do with him?" Pilate's voice echoed across the open courtyard. For a second there was stony silence and then far in the back of the crowd a lone voice yelled.

"Crucify him!"

It was the beginning point for a wave that passed over the crown until it broke against the front of Pontius Pilate's porch with a ferocity that threatened to throw Miriam back against the stone. Voice after voice joined in high chorus, screaming and shouting "Crucify him!"

Pilate turned away from the crowd and looked at the man to his left. Then, his eyes passed over Miriam for a flicker of a second. He turned to the Roman centurion.

"Isn't there some Jewish tradition that on the Passover one prisoner may be released?" The soldier shrugged his shoulders.

"I'm not sure sir."

Miriam heard the words and sensed the intent in Pilate's voice. She stepped timidly forward out of the shadows. "Excuse me, your Excellency. Among my people there is such a tradition."

Pilate's head snapped in her direction and for a second he looked at her as if she were an insect. His features softened as he listened to her.

"Are you sure, little girl?" He asked.

Once again Miriam's heart beat against the skin of her chest and her eyes went once again to the man standing on the edge of the porch. He had his back to her and she saw the stripes that were there, the blood and the flayed skin hanging from the open wounds beneath the scarlet robe. Perhaps this was his only chance for redemption.

"Yes, your Excellency. I am sure."

Roma appeared at Miriam's side. Her claw like hand clutched Miriam's shoulder. "You should not speak, flea." Miriam cringed and tears filled her eyes from the pain of Roma's grip.

"Is this true?" Pilate looked up at Roma. "You are one of them." He motioned over his shoulder at the crowd.

Roma's lips quivered and she nodded. "Yes sir."

Pilate cast one last glance at Miriam and turned to his centurion. "Bring up one of the other rebels. Bring the leader, Barabbas."

The Roman centurion marched stiffly across the porch to Pilate. "Barabbas? He's a rebel rouser. He's a murderer. Even his own people hate him. Do you think that they'll let him go?"

Pilate's eyebrows raised and he smiled. "If not, then I'm giving them a difficult decision."

Barabbas appeared through the far archway, urged on by a Roman soldier. He was shoved out into the bright sunlight at the edge of the porch. Pilate cast one glance at Miriam, their eyes meeting. "I hope you're right about this little girl or you and your guardian will pay."

Roma's grip lessened and she backed slowly away as if to put as much distance between her and Miriam as possible. Pilate walked to the front of the porch and gazed over the crowd. Like a hungry beast stalking its prey, it fell silent in anticipation. "As is your tradition, I bring before you two condemned prisoners. To honor your own traditions I will release one of them to you. Who shall it be, Jesus of Nazareth or Barabbas?"

Miriam held her breath, her clenched fists suddenly coming up to her chest. The crowd began to mumble and suddenly it once again erupted with one loud voice.

"Give us Barabbas and crucify Jesus." The sound carried over and over. Miriam slumped back against the cold stone and she felt the tears roll down her cheeks. Pilate turned abruptly and strode into the shadows near the back of the porch, rubbing his jaw.

"I don't like this. I don't like it at all. But it's not my decision. They've made their choice." He glanced at Miriam angrily and then clapped his hands together. "Child, bring me my basin."

Miriam seemed frozen for a second, pressed against the cold stone of the rock by the man's harsh glare. Then her eyes traveled from Pilate's face to the man standing at the edge of the porch. He had turned so that his back was to the crowd. The look on his face told her everything she needed to know. She did not understand what was happening or why. She saw acceptance in the man's features, a peace about what was to happen.

Miriam hurried through the open archway into Pilate's room to retrieve the basin. Roma stood in the shadows, motionless, having not moved from where she was before. Miriam stepped past her and retrieved the basin and the white cloth. She paused as something caught her eye and she glanced up at Roma's face. Were those tears on her cheeks? She hurried out onto the porch and Pilate stood at the very edge in front of the crowd. He clapped his hands and motioned to her. She stepped out into the bright sunlight. She stood poised on the edge of the porch, as if on a great chasm and the crowd threatened to swallow her whole. Pilate dipped his hands into the basin. The moment his fingers touched the clear water, blood leaked into the water. Pilate's eyes widened in amazement. Where had the blood come from? Pilate had never touched the flogged man.

"Bring me fresh water!" He hissed.

Miriam lurched with the basin back through the curtain into the darkness. She rested the bowl on the table behind Pilate's throne. But, when she looked at the water, it was clear. No blood. She poured more fresh water from the pitcher and returned to the porch. Pilate dipped his hands in again. Once again, drops of blood ran from his fingertips. He gasped and left his hands in the water. The blood disappeared.

"My towel!" He said.

Miriam placed the basin on a pedestal nearby and dried Pilate's hands. The water stained the fresh, white cloth pink. Pilate looked at his hands. He examined his fingertips.

"Again! My basin!"

She hurried over and brought the heavy bowl to him. He dipped his hands into the water slowly, gingerly. This time, there was no blood. He sighed and washed his hands, wringing them together in the water until it splashed into Miriam's face.

"My towel." Before she could move, he snatched the towel from her arm and dried his hands. "You people have made your decision and I wash my hands of this affair, do you understand?"

He threw the white cloth into the water of the basin and turned his back on the crowd, striding into the darkness of his office. Miriam stood on the edge of the porch, confused, as the Roman centurion retrieved the man to her right and led him from the porch. The crowd began to disperse and still she stood. The crowd disappeared and she was left alone on the porch. A shadow fell over her and she looked up to see Roma standing in the sunlight beside her.

"I think it's time for you to go, little girl. Pilate doesn't want to see your face again. And you can take the basin with you. He never wants to see it again. Maybe you can trade it in for some money to pay off your debt to keep you out of prison."

Miriam looked up at Roma, her eyes filled with tears, her lip trembling. "I don't understand what happened here today."

Roma's eyes traveled over the empty courtyard and came back to rest on Miriam's face. "Neither do I. Somehow that man bought you freedom from slavery. Now take the basin and go to your mother and don't ever come back to this palace again."

"Freedom?" Miriam said to the empty air around her. Was this the truth of which the man spoke? She looked down into the pink stained water of the basin soaked into the white cloth rimmed in gold thread. The wet cloth would be perfect for her mother's forehead.

Miriam emptied the rest of the water onto the floor and watched as it mixed with the blood that had trickled there from the man's back. She clutched the basin and the soaked cloth underneath her arm and ran as fast as she could for home.

CHAPTER 16

THE WIDOW

And there followed him a great company of people, and of women, which also bewailed and lamented him. But Jesus turning unto them said, "Daughters of Jerusalem, weep not for me, but weep for yourselves, and for your children. For, behold, the days are coming, in the which they shall say, 'Blessed are the barren, and the wombs that never bare, and the paps which never gave suck. Then shall they begin to say to the mountains, Fall on us; and to the hills, Cover us.'"

Luke 23:27-30 (NIV)

With a harsh, cruel motion of her hand, Hannah wiped the white paste across her face. She looked in the glass that mirrored her features. She adjusted the white paint on her face so that no skin showed. Hannah's face looked lifeless. With another sudden movement, she pasted black across her lips. Her hands snaked into the pot before her and brought out ashes that she sprinkled in her hair. Hannah whirled in the darkness of her room and grabbed a black cloak from the wooden peg by the door. She settled it around her shoulders. Next, came a black shawl draped over her head. Hannah glanced in the glass once more and approved of the harsh, ghostly figure that stood before her. It looked dead.

"I'll show them. They think that they are the best. They think that they can push me out because I'm a lonely widow. I can do as well as the rest of them. Just wait until they hear me, the old biddies."

Hannah slung open her door to the outside world and bright sunlight gushed in from the outside. She squinted in the light and casting the black shawl over her face she stepped out into the dusty, hot streets of Jerusalem.

To her left, down the road, Hannah could hear the crowd gathering. It would be in that direction that she would need to go. She hurried along pushing people roughly out of her way. One woman glanced over her shoulder, tears on her face and Hannah laughed out loud.

"You don't even know how to cry!" Hannah barked into the woman's face and pushed beyond her toward the street.

A group of women had already gathered at the side of the road. There must have been five mourners there, all dressed in black like her. Their faces painted in the white of death, their lips black slashes, their mouths opened to utter unwieldy sounds of pain and suffering. She shook her head sadly.

"They can't even scream well." Hannah muttered. She pushed through the crowd to the other side of the road and planted herself firmly in front of a large, fat man. The man mumbled gruffly behind her and she turned around.

"Leave me alone, I'm doing my job." The bitterness dripped from her voice.

Hannah glanced down the street between the two sides of the crowd to where she could see the Roman soldiers approaching. Roman soldiers. How she hated them. If it hadn't been for the Roman soldiers her husband would still be alive. But then, he had been a fool. He had sold his soul to the Romans and it was no wonder that they betrayed him. He had died at their hands. Hannah cursed his soul to Gehenna for leaving her alone in this world with no money and no way to fend for herself. Her only hope was to sell her services as a professional mourner.

By tradition women who chose to be mourners could line the funeral path. Those mourners who wailed the loudest were usually paid by the family for the job that they had performed. Hannah doubted that anybody walking down this road would have family who could pay her, but at least her presence here was good advertising. The crowd was large today and while their eyes would be fixed on the men who would walk down this road, they would also have to pass across her. If she could out scream the women across the path, they would know who was the best. The first Roman soldier made his way past them and the first prisoner stumbled beneath the weight of his cross.

Hannah went into her act, throwing herself into the dirt, groveling and screeching in a high-pitched voice. Through the struggling man's legs, she saw the other mourners wailing. None of them had thrown themselves in the dirt. Hannah proved that she could grovel with the best of them. The first prisoner had passed by and another group of Roman soldiers came into sight. One of them sneered at her and kicked sand in her face. She stood up and clinched her fist at him and then remembered the people who were watching her.

The second prisoner came in sight, stumbling beneath the load of his cross. She fell to her knees and screamed the loudest she could. Her wails threatened to drown out the mumbling of the crowd around her. The six women across the way seemed to pause and glance at her in irritation. Inwardly she smiled. She would show them she was the best.

Another group of soldiers followed the second prisoner as he made his way up the hill. Hannah waited anxiously for the third and last prisoner to appear over the crest of the hill. She saw the tip of his cross bobbing and weaving as it came over the top of the rise and then the cross piece and then the bowed head. She reached to grab the edge of her garment. This time she was going to go all the way. She was going to rip her garment in half and throw herself before the man's feet. That would win her so many contracts as a mourner she could buy bread for the next two months.

Hannah's hands paused in mid tear. The man's head was very different. It wasn't bare like the rest of them. Something was pressed around his head, like a crown. She stood there silently as the head came over the crest of the hill. The crown was not made of metal, it was made of wood. She saw red points of blood drip from edges of the crown of thorns.

How odd she thought. Why would they make a prisoner wear a crown made out of thorns? Hannah shook her head and tried to get back into her stance. Already the other group of mourners were letting loose with the loudest whooping and wailing that she had heard all day. She opened her mouth to utter another cry and this time the cry came softly at the sight in front of her.

The man's body now came into sight over the edge of the hill. He hunched over beneath the weight of the cross and Hannah could see along his back the rips and the tears from the cat-o-nine tails. The blood had hardened, and chunks of flesh were missing. She heard a wailing sound that was incredibly deep, and yet soft. She looked around to see who it was and realized it was her own voice. She pressed her hand to her mouth. How could this be? Who was this man that was beginning to move her? She shook her head and tried to draw upon her professional dignity and prepared to rend her clothes.

The man stumbled and fell forward into the dirt. When he did, blood from his back splattered through the air and she felt the warm drops of fluid hit her in the face. Tears began to form in the corners of her eyes as she looked at the man lying in the sand before her. His body was bruised and bloodied, the crown of thorns oozed blood on the edge of his hair running down to stain a perfectly seamless scarlet robe. His eyes were closed in exhaustion and pain. She fell to her knees beside him Hannah reached forward to touch his face and she drew back.

What was she doing? She was losing everything that she had worked for. Where was her good mourning technique? Why was she not wailing like the six biddies screaming their lungs out across the road?

The man's eyes opened and met hers. Hannah felt something snap inside of her and a warm flush ran inside her body. The man lifted up on his hands, his eyes turned toward her. Those eyes were filled with so much pain And beneath the pain, there was something else. She knelt closer, gazing into his eyes. There was love there. Love? How could this man love anyone? How could those eyes hold anything but the anger and resentment and hatred she felt in her heart? The coldness of her heart began to melt as she knelt before his face, and she wept. The moans that came now were genuine. The agony that she felt was real and poured from her mouth, echoing down the empty street. She reached forward with her hand and touched the man's face.

He arose slowly to his hands, then to his knees, his eyes never leaving hers. A Roman soldier beside him picked up the cross and dropped it again on his back. The man stumbled beneath the load and then he looked at her one more time.

"Daughter of Jerusalem, weep not for me, but weep for yourselves, and for your children." His words pierced her heart.

He passed Hannah by and the cries and wails that came from her now were filled with such pain and mourning that her soul was emptied of all of its bitterness. Someone tugged at her sleeve. She turned to look at the man standing beside her. He clutched in his hand several denarii.

"Good woman, you are an excellent mourner. I would like to hire you for my mother's funeral."

Hannah glanced down at the money and back at the man's

face. Her heart that had once been so hard and so cold was filled with a sadness and a sorrow that was too genuine. She shook her head as the tears blurred her eyes.

"Didn't you hear what he said? He told me to mourn no more." Hannah turned her back on the man and made her way down the street following behind the man who had taught her the true meaning of mourning.

CHAPTER 17

INTERLUDE

Then Satan entered Judas, called Iscariot, one of the Twelve.
Luke 22:3 (NIV)

*B*efore you begin the next chapter realize it may seem controversial. In 1992, God inspired me to write a play entitled, "Crosstalk". The movie "The Last Temptation of Jesus Christ" had been in the news along with the book it was based on. Let's just say the movie was far from a realistic depiction of the historical Christ. But it raised an interesting question. Was Jesus tempted to come down from the cross? Was there a bookend temptation from Satan to match that at the temptation at the beginning of Jesus' ministry? We do not know.

I cannot believe that Satan wasn't there observing the end results of his greatest efforts to thwart God's will. After all, the scriptures clearly state that Satan "entered Judas". This was a very personal involvement by Satan who normally used his demonic forces to avoid getting his "hands" dirty. What would Satan be thinking if he was watching the crucifixion? Did he have any idea the death of Jesus would not be truly final? For we know that the death and resurrection of Jesus Christ was the final blow to Satan and his plans. He is forever defeated no matter what he accomplished in the centuries since.

In response to the movie, I chose to write a play, a rather abstract play, in which Satan speaks his mind as Jesus is dying on the cross. And, Jesus' response to those thoughts were the final utterances of what he said while hanging on the cross. Did Jesus know Satan was there? Did he see Satan? Could he have heard Satan? We have no way of knowing this side of heaven. But I can speculate on what Satan may have thought as he watched in utter glee and joy what he thought would be his ultimate triumph over God's plans. And, man was he wrong!

Realize then that the next couple of chapters take dramatic license on what could have been going through the minds of those who stood on Golgotha. They watched the events unfold as Jesus Christ drew all of time and space and reality into his heart so that his unbreakable forgiveness would transcend our feeble existence and bring us mere mortals into a lasting eternal relationship with God.

CHAPTER 18

THIEVES – PART 1

Two other men, both criminals, were also led out with him to be executed.

Luke 23:32 (NIV)

I stumbled down the street bouncing from person to person. The shouts of derision and hatred echoed in my ears. Somewhere ahead was my son, Joseph. Three men were to be crucified, my son and his friend and the carpenter from Bethlehem.

Someone shoved me aside and I fell into the street. I had lost my walking stick in the confusion. A shadow loomed over me and a Roman centurion shoved me aside.

"Out of the way, street trash or you will join them on the crosses." His face twisted in anger and hatred. What was the world coming to?

Behind the centurion the carpenter from Bethlehem appeared carrying a cross. It was more than just a crosspiece. It was the entire cross! When the Romans wanted to punish someone beyond human imagining, they made them carry the much heavier completed cross up to Golgotha. The man fell beneath the weight of the cross and a woman in black came toward him. Another Roman soldier pushed her aside and struck the man with a whip.

"Get up! Carry your cross!" He shouted.

I scurried to the side of the street and huddled at the feet of the screaming crowd as the man lifted himself painfully out of the dirt. He wore a strange crown. What was it made of? Thorns? And, a crimson robe covered his shoulders.

"If you are a king, then call on your soldiers and save yourself!" A woman shouted behind me.

"Call down your holy army and save us all!" A man screamed and the crowd behind me laughed. Evil laughter. Haughty laughter. The carpenter stood up slowly beneath the cross and lifted it again on his shoulders.

"You're going to need help with that." Someone said behind me. I turned. A man in a black robe smiled at the sight before us. His features were unmarked by facial hair. His eyes were a shocking icy blue. He licked his thin lips with a very red tongue and smiled again. That smile! It was evil, unearthly. The man's head was covered with a black hood and his hands, almost skeletal, rubbed against each other in anticipation.

"I said they would betray you. I said it was a waste of time to love them." He said again. I stood slowly and followed the man's gaze to the carpenter. He was talking to Jesus of Nazareth! Who was he?

Jesus made it a dozen or so more feet up the street and fell again. I heard the black robed man gasp in pleasure and clap his hands. I stared at him. The other people around him were loud, raucous with spittle running down their chins. Their eyes were wide and round like an animal caught in a trap. But, this man, he was calm, calculated, focused. He was enjoying every minute of Jesus' misery.

The Roman soldier pointed to someone in the crowd ahead.

A man with dark skin was pulled roughly into the street and the soldier pointed to the cross.

"You! Carry his cross."

The man shook with fear but squatted down to lift the cross. His eyes met the eyes of Jesus and time seemed to stand still in that gaze.

"What are you doing?" The black robed man said loudly, marching forward to the soldier. "Don't get soft on me now."

I looked around. No one seemed to be seeing the man but me. Was I hallucinating? The soldier ignored the man in black and time moved again as the chosen man took Jesus' cross and headed up the street. Jesus stood shakily.

"You think this will buy you some time, don't you?" The black robed man said. "You're wrong. It's over and I am going to enjoy every moment of this."

Jesus ignored the man and stumbled after his cross. The man in the black robe stood motionless in the center of the street and turned and made eye contact with me. He raised an eyebrow, his piercing blue eyes boring into mine.

"You can see me?" He said.

I tried to back into the crowd, but they shoved me aside. The man advanced, his bony hands wriggling in anticipation. He stopped just short of me and his head tilted like a snake studying his prey. "How can you see me?"

"I don't know."

"Are you one of his followers? They all deserted him, of course."

"No. My son is one of the thieves to be crucified."

The man straightened and looked around him, a thin finger on his chin. "Ah, yes. He was assigned to Abbadon. I had to make sure the carpenter would be crucified with the lowliest riff raff in Jerusalem. Add insult to injury! Your son, hmmm. We'll be harvesting his soul soon." He looked back at me and rubbed his hands in anticipation. "Unless you'd like to make a deal. Your soul for his? I can see that he never gets put on the cross."

My skin began to crawl as the crowd dissipated around me following the show up the hill. My heart raced and my mouth grew dry. Could it be? I had heard tales of this creature my entire life. He was in the Scriptures. My mother had scared me with tales of his evil doings. For a fleeting second, I considered what he had offered. My soul to save my son?

"Are you Satan?"

The man stiffened and his mouth opened in an inhuman wail. I put my hands over my ears. Fiery anger filled his eyes. "Do not call me that!" He stepped toward me and paused. He looked me up and down and reached out one of his bony hands to almost touch me. "My name is Lucifer, the morning star, the apple of God's eye. I was His favorite. Why can I not touch you? I thought you were not one of His followers."

"I am not."

"But, something in your past, perhaps? You've been around him before this time?" His eyes filled with interest and he leaned close to me. His breath was cold and smelled of dirt and decay and tombs. "You were there, weren't you? At his birth? I tried to find them, but they were hidden away with their family. In what? A manger? It was you who protected them so he could be born?"

Satan stepped back and glared at me. "I'm wasting my time on you. You are protected. Too bad your son isn't. Now, if you'll excuse me, I am about to have the time of my life!" He disappeared from sight. I shook my head in amazement and continued painfully up the road to Golgotha. I heard a familiar voice long before I topped the rise.

"Father! Save me! Don't let them do this to me!"

I tried to run forward toward the sound of my son's voice, but the centurion blocked my way. He shoved me down onto the hard, hot rocks of the hill of Golgotha.

"Are you running to your cross?" He glared at me.

"It's my son!" I sobbed. "He's calling for me."

The centurion shrugged. "They usually cry out for their mothers."

I stood shakily to my feet. "Please! May I tell him I love him?"

The centurion shook his head. "You can tell him anything you want once he's hanging on the cross."

Satan appeared from behind the centurion and glanced in my direction. "It's you again. I thought so. Given any more thought to my proposal?"

"No! I can still save him." I said.

"Oh, I don't think so. But, just to prolong your agony," He leaned forward and whispered in the centurion's ear. The centurion blinked and focused on me.

"I'll give you a few minutes before we haul him up on his cross piece." The centurion barked something in their language to the two soldiers working over my son. They glanced at each other and then stood away. I hurried across the rough ground and knelt beside my son. He was spread eagled on the cross piece. Nails had been driven through his hands.

"Son!" I said, tears pouring from my eyes.

"Father! I was so wrong. I don't want to die a martyr's death. I had so much of life to live." He cried and screamed in agony when he moved his hands.

"It's the nerve in the wrist." The cold whisper came in my ear. "Strategically placed nails not only anchor the body through the wrist bones, but they impinge on the main nerve from the hand. You see if the nail is merely between the hand bones, the weight of the body rips through the muscle and tendons. But, the wrist bones are tightly connected and one can put a nail point in the mid palm and then angle it through the wrist bones into the wood. Like hanging something on your wall. Ingenious, don't you think?"

I closed my eyes and tried to ignore Satan. "Son, I can save you." I said.

Joseph glanced at me and his crying stopped. "What?"

"It's a simple exchange." Satan said over my shoulder.

Joseph's focus shifted to my shoulder. "Who is that?"

"You can see him?" I said glancing over my shoulder. Satan stood over us, his bony hands weaving and gesturing. His tongue darted out of his mouth.

"I am the one who can give your father what he wants. I can convince the centurion to free you." Satan said.

"No! We tried bribery!" Joseph gasped in pain. "If the soldiers let us off the cross, they go up."

"Not if your father agrees to take your place." Satan smiled. "A soul for a soul."

Joseph blinked furiously and focused on me. "What? You would sell you soul to this thing to save me?"

"A father will do anything to save his son." I said, my heart sinking. I could already feel the nails in my palms.

"No!" He screamed. "Centurion, I am ready for the cross!"

I threw myself over Joseph's body. "Son! I've lived my life. You have so much ahead of you."

His eyes were dead level with mine. "Father, you love me too much. I was blind to that. Now, I must face the consequences of my choices. You have to take care of Mother."

Rough hands grabbed my arms and pulled me away. I fought against them, but my strength was insufficient, and two soldiers dragged me away and tossed me down the slope. I rolled and tumbled through the rocks and dirt until I came to rest against a boulder. I sat up painfully, tears streaming from eyes as the soldiers hoisted the crosspiece carrying my son up and let it slam into place on the upright piece. I tried to scream but my voice was gone. They stripped away his loin cloth and began to nail his feet to the upright piece. My son's screams rose above the clamor of the crowd.

"They nail the feet so when the victim's push up to breathe out, the pain is excruciating." Satan knelt beside me. "You see, with their arms upstretched, they can't blow out their air. They suffocate with a lung full of air! Isn't it delicious! Every breath is agony! It's amazing what you people can think up. With my inspiration, of course."

"Get away from me, Satan!" I shouted.

Satan stood up stiffly and stepped back. Surprise filled his eyes. "You can't tell me what to do!"

I stood up slowly and advanced on him. I put out a hand to touch him. "I can reach out and touch you. You said I was protected. If that is so, then you can no longer torment me."

He stepped back and raised an eyebrow in surprise. "I'm bored with you and your son anyway. I have bigger fish to fry." He gestured toward the center cross as it slammed into the ground in one piece.

Jesus of Nazareth, naked and covered with blood groaned in agony. "I have dreamt of this day since my failure in the Garden. He sends His son, his physical manifestation into MY realm and now I will have MY way with him." Satan walked toward the crosses and I followed, forcing myself to focus on the body of my son gasping for breath on the cross.

Satan stopped, raised his arms and turned slowly, taking in the sights. "What a gorgeous, wonderful, exhilarating day! Look at that sun. What a scorcher it is going to be! Not a cloud in sight! Yes, a wonderful day. In fact, the best day of my life! You just can't beat a day like today." He paused and faced the center cross. "Yoo hoo. Hey, you up there? Yes, you. It's me again. I'm back. You don't look so good. In fact, you look worse than you did the last time we met face to face. You remember. In the wilderness I tried to warn you. But, no, you wouldn't listen!" He paced back and forth; his eyes focused on the center cross.

"And now, look at you. Nailed to a tree. Out here in the hot sun with all these people staring at you. You should have listened to me." He paused and glanced at me and then at my son. "Well, let's see what we can do about it. You know, you don't have to stay up there. All you got to do is say the word, no, just THINK the word and the armies of heaven will come to your rescue. They would crush these pitiful humans like a bunch of ants."

Was I watching the spiritual match up of the ages? Jesus was just a carpenter. Why would Satan taunt him so? Unless Jesus was truly the Messiah! And, not the conquering warrior we had all waited for. What had the Magi said? A suffering, servant leader? Jesus was going to die on the cross! What kind of leadership was that? Why would God send down the Messiah only to have him die at the hands of his own creation?

Satan turned around and surveyed the crowd around him. Near the foot of the cross the soldiers and a lone man in a robe were casting dice over the remnants of Jesus' possessions. How could God love such as us? I glanced up and Satan's gaze fixed on me.

"Yes, I said pitiful. Like your son." He turned back to the center cross. "Just look at them. Standing around weeping and screaming. The poor things. And, just a minute ago they were yelling 'Crucify him.' So fickle. And you want to die for them. What a waste. They'll never change, and you know it. You've seen it all. And, to tell, the truth, I've seen some of it, too. That's why I am here. Now. To try and talk some sense into you. I was going to greet you in the Garden of Gethsemane, but there were those pesky angels flying around like a swarm of mosquitoes."

Angels? I blinked and looked around me at the weeping, mourning people clustered on the hillside. Were some of them angels in disguise? Had God sent angels to minister to his only Son? If not, why not? It was as if Jesus HAD to die! But, why?

Satan tapped a spindly finger on his chin. "But, here, you're on your own, buddy. Left high and dry. No one's shoulder to lean on. Except, of course, mine. I'll make you a deal. You just curse these pitiful human insects down here and we'll get you down off of that cross and into a nice, warm bath in no time."

The soldiers and the man at the foot of the cross suddenly erupted into action. Another story was unfolding before my eyes. And, then Jesus said something that changed the world.

CHAPTER 19

THE ROBE — PART 2

Two other men, both criminals, were also led out with him to be executed. When they came to the place called the Skull, they crucified him there, along with the criminals—one on his right, the other on his left. Jesus said, "Father, forgive them, for they do not know what they are doing." And they divided up his clothes by casting lots.

Luke 23:32-34 (NIV)

 $\mathcal{N}$ athan stood at the edge of the crowd as the cross rose against the afternoon sun. The shadow of the cross inched its way over the crowd and fell upon his face, eclipsing the hot sunlight. He tried to see the man's face in the shadow of the cross, but he could not. The man was naked. His arms were held by spikes penetrating the flesh of his wrists and his feet. Against the bright sunlight he could see the shadow of the crown of thorns still upon his head, but the robe was gone.

Nathan stood transfixed in the shadow of the cross. The mass of humanity touching his shoulders, the wailing of the widows around him mixed with the roar of the crowd crying for blood.

He tore his eyes away from the figure on the cross and studied the barren space around the base of the three crosses. To one side he could see the Roman soldiers, laughing and patting each other on the back. Lying at the foot of the cross was the wooden mallet stained with blood and the loin cloth from the man's waist. Nearby lay his son's robe in the dust and the dirt of Golgotha.

Nathan stepped across the empty space until he stood face to face with the Roman centurion.

"What do you want? Get back in the crowd and get out from under these crosses before I nail you to one of them." The centurion said.

Nathan was afraid for the first time in his life. It was a different kind of fear from what he felt at the height of a gambling session. Always then, there was the rush of adrenaline, the glow of success that always rode the crest of failure, just before he won that great last gamble. This felt different. If he lost to this gamble, he would lose his life. He licked his lips and motioned toward the robe lying in the dirt.

"Good centurion, you took my son's robe from me. Isn't there anything I can do to get it back? What is to become of it?"

The Centurion glanced beyond Nathan at the robe lying on the ground. "I haven't given it much thought. Perhaps one of the other soldiers would like to have it. We could tear it into pieces."

"No!" Nathan's voice sounded in the sudden silence that hovered at the foot of the cross. "I mean, why not cast lots? Let your men cast lots to see who wins the ownership of the robe. And since it was my idea, might I also join in?"

Nathan gave his eyes their best twinkle, his smile, the best winning smile he could find. He put on his poker face but in his heart, there was fear.

Another Roman soldier stepped up beside the centurion. "So

Nathan wants to gamble again, does he? And what do you have to offer in exchange for this robe when you lose?"

Nathan glanced up at the Roman centurion. In the back of his mind he heard his wife's voice pleading. He saw the disrespect in his son's eyes. How could he have been such a fool? All he could see now was the robe, the years of effort that his wife had put into it, the proud expression on his son's face as he stepped into manhood. He had to have the robe.

"If I lose, then you can put me on a cross, right now, beside these three men."

The Roman centurion laughed. "I could do that right now anyway, you piece of trash. Rome is sovereign here and what Rome says, Rome can do."

Nathan licked his lips and then rubbed at his face and glanced once again at the robe lying at the foot of the cross. "If I lose and you nail me to the cross, then I will denounce my God and even as I die, I will proclaim the sovereignty of Caesar and the wisdom of Pilate to my dying breath."

The Roman centurion nodded. "That would be impressive. It would also be degrading to you. Very well, you may join in as we cast lots. I look forward to you pleading to Caesar for intervention from your cross."

Nathan backed away slowly, his heart pounding and he turned to kneel beside the robe lying in the dust. His hand went out and touched the soft cloth. He noticed that there were streaks of dried blood from the man's back and as he examined the cloth, he felt something warm drop on his right hand. He studied the drop of blood on the back of his hand and his eyes turned upwards to the man nailed to the cross. The man's eyes fixed with his and for a moment he felt the fear lift from his heart.

"My God, for this one time, smile down upon your servant and give me the odds to win this robe."

Nathan stood and crossed to where the group of soldiers

squatted in the sand. He reached into his pocket and brought out the well-worn dice that he was going to throw. There were four Roman soldiers huddled in the dust and Nathan handed the robe to the Roman Centurion.

"Here's the robe, your Excellency. You be the judge of who wins and who loses."

They threw their first dice and one Roman soldier swore as his dice turned upwards in the dust. There was laughter around him and he reached into the circle of men and grasping his dice, he turned his back on them. One by one Nathan faced them down throwing his dice, each time breathing a silent prayer, the dice fell in the dust. One last soldier remained. He and the first Roman soldier that he had seen that day faced off over the robe. This was the deciding moment. One by one the others had been eliminated and his luck had held out. He glanced one more at the cross and at the man hanging there and with his eyes closed he threw the dice.

"Father, forgive them for they know not what they do." The words echoed from the man on the cross and suddenly the wind stirred at the foot of the crosses. Nathan looked down at his dice and he noticed the Roman soldier across from him had his eyes fixed on the cross. He reached to the man's dice and adjusted them and then adjusted his own.

The Roman soldier looked down and swore as he saw that he had lost. Nathan stood shakily and he glanced over at the Roman centurion. "I've won the robe fair and square. May I have it?"

The Roman centurion's eyes burrowed into his. "You cheated. I saw you change the dice." His face was fixed in stern, dark anger.

Nathan was convinced that both of their faces had been turned towards the cross. The man's words had stung them, confused them and even through the anger on the centurion's face he could see the confusion still lurking.

"You weren't looking at me. You were looking at the cross, just like I was. I didn't cheat. The robe is rightfully mine and you know it."

Nathan prepared himself for the onslaught of the anger of the Roman soldier but there was none. Quietly, the Roman centurion handed him the robe. His face was filled with confusion, not anger.

"Get out of here." Were his only words.

Nathan's heart pounded as he held the robe to his chest. He felt the pressure of the dice in his right hand and he cast one last look at them and then hurled them in the dust, in the dirt at the foot of the cross. He had cheated. But the pain of the cheating was nothing as he stood at the foot of the cross with the robe clutched against his chest. He studied the face of the man that hung there. Yes, he had cheated, but he had also won back the robe and the trust of his family. More importantly than that, he had this day received forgiveness.

CHAPTER 20

THIEVES — PART 2

I am poured out like water, and all my bones are out of joint. My heart has turned to wax; it has melted within me. My mouth is dried up like a potsherd, and my tongue sticks to the roof of my mouth; you lay me in the dust of death. Dogs surround me, a pack of villains encircles me; they pierce my hands and my feet. All my bones are on display; people stare and gloat over me. They divide my clothes among them and cast lots for my garment.

　　　Psalms 22:14-18 (NIV)

When Jesus uttered those incredible words of forgiveness, Joseph glanced at me just as Satan screamed in agony. He held his hands to his ears.

"NO, NO, NO! Now you've gone and done it. You've offered forgiveness to them all!" He whirled in pain and halted, facing the crosses. "What is wrong with you! Can't you see what they've done to you? Are you blind? You're hanging from a cross! How in the world can you possibly forgive them?"

How could he forgive the soldiers who nailed him to the

cross or those of us who lauded his arrival into Jerusalem only to call for his death? How could he forgive my son? How could he forgive me? The old anger grew and stoked within me. I could never forgive the soldiers who had nailed my brother to a cross so many years ago or my son today. How could I?

Satan's voice came to me, soft and seductive. "Oh, I guess you're going to blame me? Right? Wrong, buster! Remember, they made the choice in the garden. All I did was educate them. All I've ever been is an encourager."

I blinked. Satan was right. We had made the decisions, soldiers and victims alike. But, not without provocation from the enemy of peace and love; this creature who stood before me. I wished I could blame him for all of our calamity. But the truth was, we were the ones who made the choices. And we had to live with that. But, find forgiveness? Never!

Satan had wandered over to a table covered with whips and mallets and nails. He reached out and touched a clay jar. "Sure is a hot day in the old town today! That sun makes it as hot as, well, you know where." He chuckled and the low, evil echo of his voice sent chills down my spine. "Bet you haven't had anything to eat or drink in quite some time. Must be pretty thirsty." He motioned to the jar. "What's this, you ask? Why it's a wonderful jar of wine. Cool, refreshing, thirst quenching. Wouldn't you just love a taste?"

I glanced past Satan at the center cross. Jesus' gaze was upward toward the sky. He had not made eye contact with Satan. I wasn't even sure if he was hearing the creature.

"I thirst." Jesus said quietly.

I jerked as if stabbed with a sword. He was thirsty? Human, hurting, bleeding. How could that be so if he was divine? I shifted my gaze to Joseph gasping for breath as his eyes focused on Jesus.

"Yes!" Satan hissed as he walked over to a soldier. He whispered in the man's ear. "Why don't you give him something to wet his whistle, soldier boy."

The soldier swatted at his ear as if a fly had buzzed him. He retrieved a wine flagon from his belt.

"NO, not the wine. Give him something that'll taste terrible. Like vinegar." Satan motioned to the clay jar. The soldier dropped the flagon back to his waist and crossed to the jar. He poured some of it onto a sponge and affixed it to the end of a long reed. He walked over to the center cross and lifted the sponge toward Jesus' lips.

"See how you like that." Satan said out loud. "Why don't you perform another miracle? Change the vinegar into wine. Show the boys a good time." Jesus ignored the sponge and Satan laughed. "I told you, you wouldn't make it. You're weakening. After all, you're only HUMAN." He crossed his arms. "Listen, I got you with the thirst business and I'll just keep after it until you give in, so give it up! Hop on down from that cross and lets you and I plan the future of this cute, little planet. Just think of the things we could do together."

Two figures appeared at my side walking slowly toward the center cross. At first, I thought the woman might be Rachel come to see our son. As I gazed at her face twisted in pain, wet with tears I recognized her. It was Mary! The mother of Jesus. I had passed her many times when I went to Joseph's house to work on the chair. I gasped in shock and sat back on a boulder. I moaned in pain at the realization that my life had come full circle. What had one of the gifts been? Myrrh! For embalming? And what were the other two? Yes, gold for a king. And Frankincense for a priest. I lifted my gaze to the center cross.

Was he there even now interceding on our behalf? Was he shedding his blood just as the blood of the lambs were shed for the atonement of sin? Was this God's plan? Mary was accompanied by a younger man and they paused before the cross. The younger man's shoulders heaved in sobbing and he clung to

Mary with all his strength. I wanted to run to her, to ask he what was happening? Surely, she knew. If this was some grand divine plan, she had to know.

Satan stood far from the pair, but his face turned toward me and he held out one of his pale hands toward Mary and her companion. "Oh, my heart is breaking in two. Will you look at these two people. Have you ever seen such a sorrowful sight? John, the beloved." He spat the last word onto the ground. "Well, there's no accounting for taste. And, his sweet, little mother, Mary. You were there, weren't you? When he was born." Satan pointed to the cross. He frowned and feigned a sorrowful expression.

"Just look at this. What is wrong with this picture? I can tell you. Jesus in not in the picture." Satan glanced back at the center cross. "What in the world are these two people, the dearest people in all the world, going to do without you? They NEED you. Face it. Joseph is dead. So, who is going to take care of poor Mary? And John can't let you out of his sight. He'll be lost without you. Who is going to look after them when you're dead and gone? But I can help you with that little dilemma. Come on down off that cross. You can do it and take care of these two people you love so much."

Jesus' upward gaze drifted down slowly and he looked at Mary. "Dear woman, here is your son. John, here is your mother."

A roar of inhuman rage erupted from Satan. Mary and John heard nothing. I alone was witness to this heinous temptation. For that was what it was! Satan did not want Jesus to die! He wanted him to come down off the cross! Why?

"Give me a break! Any more of this fawning sentimentality and I'm going to vomit. I can't believe him!" Satan looked at me. "After the way they treated him, he still won't condemn them." Satan's eyes widened as he studied me. "Ah, I have the key, now." He turned toward the cross. "What about these two poor wretches on either side of you? Common thieves. The lowest of the low. Vermin. Not worthy of your attention. Why, I wouldn't give them the time of day and here you are keeping their good company."

My heart fell at the words and I looked once again at my son, straining for breath on his cross. Satan pointed at me. "One of them is his son! A common thief. You have been nailed between two criminals! What does that make you?" Satan walked over and stood beneath Joseph's cross. "How can you possibly care anything for humanity when you are surrounded by such pitiful excuses for men?"

Satan walked over to the other thieves' cross. "You. If this man is the Messiah, why are the two of you still on the cross?"

Joseph's comrade gasped for breath and his face twisted not in pain but in anger. "Aren't you the Messiah? Save yourself and us! Right, Joseph. If he is the Messiah, he can call on his troops and end this. Now!" The man gasped for breath.

Joseph looked over at his comrade. "How can you say that?"

"It's what we lived for. It's what we're dying for. We were loyal to the death. The least he can do is save us." His comrade gasped again. "Save us, you fool!"

Joseph looked down toward me, his chest heaving and for a second seemed to see Satan. He looked past him at me, and his eyes were filled with tears and pain and regret. He mouthed something I could not hear. I drew closer. He said it again. "Father, forgive me. I love you. I was wrong." Although the sound did not come, what he said was unmistakable and drove a stake through my heart. I groaned in pain.

Wasn't Joseph's comrade right? I stepped forward. Yes, I looked toward Jesus. Yes, please save them both and save us all, I thought. But before the words could make it to my lips, Joseph cried out in anger, his head tilted so he could look across the bleeding body of Jesus to his friend.

"Don't you fear God," he said, "since you are under the same sentence?" His chest heaved as he tried to speak. "We are punished justly, for we are getting what our deeds deserve. But this man has done nothing wrong." His gaze shifted to the face of Jesus, turned upward toward heaven. Jesus lowered his gaze to meet that of my son!

"No!" Satan screamed and I flinched. "Don't look at him like that. What is wrong with you? They both hate your guts. Can't you see. He's lying to you. He's delirious from the heat. He doesn't know what he is saying, claiming he deserves punishment and you don't. Don't listen to him."

Joseph cast one look in my direction and then back at Jesus. "Jesus, remember me when you come into your kingdom."

Kingdom? Jesus was king, right? More than the King of the Jews. He was the King of Kings!

Jesus spoke and the words trembled in the air; the world shuddered at the utterance and the ground shook with the power of his forgiveness. "Truly I tell you, today you will be with me in paradise."

"No, no, no, no, no!" Satan screeched as I fell to my knees. Joseph continued to look on Jesus as his friend let loose with more profanity.

Satan started pacing quickly, his hands dancing in anxiety. He paused before a woman. "You! Make fun of him. NOW! And, you," he moved among other members of the crowd. "Remember he claimed to be the king of the Jews. Remember! Just moments ago, you wanted to crucify him. Where is your bloodlust? Your passion? Let's get with the program, people. Let's live up to your potential. Come on!"

The crowd began to converge, moving together as one organism. They began to shout, "If you are the King of the Jews, come down from the cross!" And, "If you are Elijah, prophecy!"

I felt sick and slumped to the ground as they milled around me. I looked up at Joseph and his head rested on his chest. He had given up. Could I blame him? He had just come face to face with the King of Kings, the Messiah, God among us and Jesus had promised him Paradise!

Satan paced before me and I glanced up at his fierce, icy blue eyes. "That's more like it. Let him have it. You want to suffer, then so be it. Here they are.The people you want to die for. I can tell you they betrayed you now and they'll keep on betraying you. And you know it! Because, I'll be there all the way." He stood in the midst of the clamoring crowd, gesturing, almost dancing. "Look at them. See any love in their faces? They're just animals! Thirsting for your blood. All of them. Especially that one that sat at the table with you. The one that betrayed you with a kiss."

I sat on the ground for what seemed like hours. After a while, the crowd began to lessen and their voices grew silent. They wandered away. Satan had been triumphant!

"You!" Satan squatted before me. "What did it feel like to be betrayed by your own brother?"

I flinched. How did he know about my brother? Satan smiled. "How did it feel to be betrayed by your own son?" Satan stood slowly as if holding center stage. "I wonder how he," Satan gestured over his shoulder at the center cross, "Felt to be betrayed by a kiss? What did it feel like to have one of his closest friends turn against him? And what did it feel like when Peter, his Rock, cursed him around the campfire?"

I glanced up at that. Peter? I had heard stories of the fisherman. But he had betrayed Jesus? How many of his disciples had betrayed him? John had been the only one I had seen here at the cross.

Satan continued, pacing back and forth. "Just where are they, anyway? Where are all his friends? Where are all his followers who vowed to stand by him to the death? WHERE is God?"

I looked up at the sky where Jesus' gaze was fixed. Where was God? On this most terrible day, where was God?

Satan paused and smiled turning slowly to the cross. "You're human, Jesus. Right now, you're more human than you have ever been. You know why? Because you are about to die. When you were God did you ever imagine what it would be like to die? And not only that, but you are going to die alone. No one here loves you. No one here has volunteered to die in your place. Look up. Tell me, Son of Man, can you still see God?"

The voice of Jesus thundered through the air with the impact of a sudden storm. "My God, My God, why have you forsaken me?"

Clouds began to form in the sky, boiling and churning. I felt the ground tremble beneath me and stood shakily to my feet. People in the crowd began to murmur and I felt a drop of cold rain hit me in the forehead.

"Yes, yes. That's it!" Satan raised his fists in triumph. "He has forsaken you. He has turned his back on you. He broke all of his promises. He left you here to die alone. How does it feel, Jesus? How does it feel?" He rubbed his hands together. "How sad. There's only one person that can help you. ME. And, kind, compassionate soul that I am, I'm going to make you an offer you can't refuse. So why don't we make a deal. Just give it all up, right now and I'll welcome you with open arms." Satan walked toward the center cross. Roman soldiers were standing still, their gaze fixed on Jesus. The centurion stood stock still, silent audience to the confrontation of the ages.

"Just think back to all the good times you had. Wouldn't you like to be able to roam the earth with me? We could be pals. Buddies. I can give it all back to you. Forget all this mission of love garbage. You don't have to finish what you set out to do. Just come with me."

Jesus writhed in agony one last time and his head slumped toward his chest as he said quietly, "It is finished."

Satan halted his pacing and touched his chin with a finger. "Yeah, it is finished. It's a done deal. You have my word on it. I'll take care of you. Just hop on down, now. Give me your soul,

Jesus, and we'll live happily ever after. Don't worry about these silly, helpless, sheep."

Jesus' eyes opened wide and he gazed out over the crowd. Satan froze. "What did I say? Why are you looking at them that way? They're sheep, I tell you. Stupid, brainless sheep." He hurried over to stand beneath the cross as rain began to pour from the sky. Lightning tore the clouds and thunder rolled across the hillside. "What did I say? Sheep? What's wrong with sheep?"

Sheep? My thoughts went back to that night on the hillside when angels proclaimed joy to all men. What had one of the shepherds say to me? They were going to see the child who had been born in a manger. Of course a lamb would be born in a manger, one of them had said. I looked at Jesus stretched out on the cross. Was he the perfect lamb slain for the ultimate sacrifice? Gold, Frankincense, and Myrrh all pointed to a king who would become the intercessor high priest offering the ultimate sacrifice for all of our sins with HIS death! I fell to my knees as the implications passed over me. I looked once again on my son. His eyes were open wide and he was staring right at me. His body moved up and down with each painful breath and he mouthed something. I blinked. What had he said?

I was back on the rooftop with Rachel and my young Joseph. I had stretched out my hands and said, "I love you this much and more than I can reach." Joseph had mirrored my gestured and merely said, "Da."

I looked back at my son and my eyes filled with tears. He mouthed it again, "I love you this much and more than I can reach." His arms were outstretched by means other than his own doing but the meaning was the same. And then, Joseph looked over at Jesus. I swallowed and looked at the Lamb of God. He loved us this much and more than he could reach!

Loved us enough to die for us? His outstretched arms reaching around the world for us? I wept.

Satan was chattering on. "Look, Jesus, why don't you just ignore these people here and pay attention to me. No, don't look at the guards. They're Romans for crying out loud! They hate you!"

Satan paused and his face filled with worry. "That's right. There was that parable you told the crowd. Sheep. Yeah, I never should have said that word. You like being a shepherd, don't you? Wasn't there a parable you told? Looking for the lost sheep. Leaving the 99 behind to go look for the one? Well, that's pretty stupid, if you ask me. I could eat all 99 of them before you get back."

I flinched when he said the word "eat" and glared at this vile creature who dared to desecrate these holy proceedings. He glanced back at me and licked his lips. "Did I say I could eat them? Just a slip of the tongue. I would never do that. And you would make a good shepherd. Just let me help you find them. We can look for them together. Yeah, that's the ticket. Just you and me."

Jesus slowly turned his gaze upward, toward heaven, toward the God who had abandoned him, away from the prince of this world. Satan screeched. "Wait, wait! Don't look up there. He's not there, I told you. He turned his back, remember."

Jesus spoke quietly but the words poured forth over the sound of rain and thunder. "Father, into YOUR hands I commit my spirit." His head slumped onto his chest. Satan fell to his knees.

"NOOOOOOO!" The ground shook and I fell. The remaining crowd hurried away as the sky opened up and the world was swallowed by utter darkness. Wind roared around me and I hugged the earth. Somewhere up there my son was dying on his cross. Up there, God's son had died on the cross. It seemed like an eternity until nature grew tired of the outpouring of its outrage and sorrow. The wind began to die down and the thunder grew silent. The darkness lifted and a pale, gray pall hung over everything. It was if the universe had died and now lay listless and lifeless all around me.

Satan stood up slowly, his hands coming off from his ears. He looked up at the body of Jesus. "You may think you've won this round, buddy. But this is far from over. You're about to end up the way of all flesh. In a tomb. Signed, sealed, delivered! Yeah, they're going to bury you deep in a tomb in shadows and darkness and that is where I reside. And, who is going to believe your words. No one was paying attention when you told them! Your believers are scattered to the four winds. You're dead. It's over. No one will ever believe you are the Son of God."

The centurion walked slowly up to the foot of the cross and stood right beside Satan. He took off his helmet and the dying wind tossed his hair. He wiped tears from his face. "Surely, this man was the Son of God."

Satan stiffened and glared at the centurion. "Oh, shut up!" Casting one last contemptuous look in my direction, he disappeared. The centurion glanced down at me and offered his hand. A centurion offered his hand to a Judean! I took his hand and he pulled me up from the miry clay of the Golgotha hillside and we both stood in the presence of the King of Kings.

CHAPTER 21

THE JANITOR

At that moment the curtain of the temple was torn in two from top to bottom.

Matthew 27:51 (NIV)

*L*evi pushed the broom across the worn tiles, straining to get at the blood. *Skritch, skritch, skritch.* A sound he had come to endure, repeated all day, every day for the last twenty years. My, how filthy the floor was. Especially after yesterday's record crowd. Again, he scratched at the blood soaked deep into the mortar between the tiles. Black, aged, dried from years of shed blood, the tiles would never be clean. The blood could never be removed. It was there forever. And every day, the people came, strewing dirt and straw and leaves across his carefully scrubbed floor. And every evening, he cleaned. *Skritch, skritch, skritch.*

Today, he had been fortunate. The usual crowds were gone. The vast chamber empty. And, the chief priest of the inner holy place had allowed him this one brief time to clean. He was never to have entered this space. He was unworthy, the priest had informed him. But the tiles had to be cleaned and the priest was above such indignity. And so, he had waited until the crowds thinned and left him alone before the open doors of the inner holy place reserved for the most special of Jehovah God's priests.

The people, he thought. They were all out *there*, watching the show. He did not complain. It gave him the opportunity to finish his task earlier. Perhaps tonight, he would get home before sunset.

Levi paused at the marble steps that led up to the curtain. Leaning against his broom, his eyes traveled up the great expanse of cloth. It hung from golden hooks; its velvety folds thick and impenetrable. Deep maroon cloth rustled thickly in the breeze that stirred in the temple, gold thread gleaming in the light of hanging braziers.

He smiled as he gave into his daily fantasy. In his mind, he walked up to the curtain, hands eager, hands strong. He grasped the thick, coarse cloth and he pulled with all his might. With a great rending sound, the curtain tore from bottom to top and he hurled the remnants aside.

Levi did not know what he would find inside if his fantasy were to ever become reality. He *could* not know. These thoughts bordered on blasphemy as it was. To imagine Yahweh seated on the altar was going too far. After all, he was unworthy!

He stepped up the stairs and glancing around to insure that no priests were watching, reached out his trembling hand to touch the fabric. It seemed to shudder at his touch, as if fearing him.

What lay beyond? He thought. He would never know. The priest forever stood between him and God. Only the priest could carry his sacrifice to the mercy seat of God. Only a man could bridge the gap.

Levi stepped down from the curtain and walked across the

huge chamber, his footsteps echoing. Outside, he heard thunder cascade against the roof. Rain pattered on the closed windows. Lightning leaked through the cracks, spilling sharp edged shadows onto the clean tiles. Suddenly, the great doors flew open. Wind and rain hurtled into the room. His eyes were drawn to the distant hill where the people who normally filled the temple waited. Where the priests who stood before God waited. Where a cross rose against the sky. Where the world waited.

Now, there was a man who knew how to clear out a temple, he thought. Levi had watched the man wield the cat-of-nine-tails like a sword of God as he had chased the money changers away. And the priests had nailed the carpenter to a tree. *They* had. The men who bridged the gap between he and God had nailed a good man to a cross. Because he was unworthy!

Levi turned back to the curtain, his heart filled with resentment, hatred, anger. Silently, he cursed the priests and their lofty words; he cursed the curtain that stood between he and God; and he cursed the people, like himself, who had stood by and let an innocent man die. A man who had claimed to be their savior.

The ground suddenly began to shake, and Levi stumbled, his broom clattering against the tiled floor. Light began to fill the chamber. He squinted against the brightness and searched for its source.

The light gushed from behind the curtain. Levi watched in amazement as the top of the curtain moved, lifted as if gripped by unseen hands. The sound began, a groaning that penetrated to his very soul. He fell to his knees, his hands clasped to his ears as the curtain tore. It tore from top to bottom, hurled away, exposing the brilliant white light from within. He squinted, eyes nearly shut, and for a fleeting moment saw a great figure in the light, seated on the mercy seat of God. Was it the man on the cross? How? Only the worthiest could enter the Holy of Holies and this man somehow had left his cross behind and had entered the Holiest of places and sat on the mercy seat! He smiled. Now, who was unworthy?

Just as suddenly as it had come, the light was extinguished. Levi stood shakily to his feet in the eerie silence that followed. He walked across the tiled floor, now littered with bits of fabric and gold thread to the stairs leading up to the curtain. It was gone, cast aside like grave cloth. The Holy of Holies lay within, dark, shadowy, yet exposed to the world. God no longer needed the curtain. Man no longer needed the priest. The priests were unworthy! Only the man from the cross was worthy and he had this day bridged the gap between ordinary, unworthy man and God.

Levi picked up his broom and returned to the open doors. Outside, the rain had stopped. Across the wind-swept city, sunlight chased shadows as the clouds receded. Upon the lofty hill, a lone shaft of sunlight fell on the central cross.

"Yes," He smiled. "He really knows how to clean a temple."

CHAPTER 22

THE UNWELCOME VISITOR

The earth shook, the rocks split and the tombs broke open. The bodies
of many holy people who had died were raised to life.
   Matthew 27:51b-52 *(NIV)*

A knock at the door. Manasseh looked up from the darkness of the room. The knock came again, insistent, unrelenting. Fear filled his heart and he shuddered. Outside, the sky hung like clotted blood. Rain cascaded from swollen clouds, and the earth trembled as if in labor. He did not want to open the door. He did not want to embrace the unknown. He huddled closer to the meager light of his lamp, pulling his cloak about him against the cool, damp air.

Who was at the door? A friend? Unlikely. A stranger? Perhaps. A foe? Certainly. In these times, to answer the knock at the door was folly. It might let in death.

Rap, rap, rap.

"Manasseh, let me in." A faint voice. He glanced up from his corner at the roughhewn wood of the door. Thunder shook the walls again. Could it be? Impossible! He stood shakily and crossed to the door. His hand, shaking with fear, reached to the latch.

The door swung open on a gust of rain-filled wind and she stood there. White linen draped her figure, hanging from her head, wet with rain. Her face gleamed in the lamp light with moisture and she stepped into the warmth of his home.

"Manasseh." Her voice was soft.

Manasseh fell back away from the door, stumbled on the soft rug, fell against the table. The lamp light guttered in the wind and the room was cast into stark shadows. Lightning spilled in through the door, knife edged, cutting away the blackness.

"Leah?" He mumbled, his hand to his mouth.

She moved past him to the lamp and orange light filled the room again. "Close the door," She said.

He shook his head in confusion as he shut the door against the wind and rain. "I do not understand."

She turned to him, crossing the dirt floor gracefully. The white linen fell away from her head and he saw her face, soft, radiant. Her eyes glowed with life, her cheeks ruddy.

"I came back to tell you." She reached out to touch his cheek.

Manasseh pulled away fearfully, his fingers touching the spot on his cheek where her warm hand had caressed. "How can this be?" He whispered, feeling the hardness of the door bite into his back.

"I cannot stay long." She came nearer. "Why are you hiding?"

"Hiding?" He managed through numb lips. "Have you seen what is going on out there?" He motioned toward the door.

"Yes."

"We all had to run. Hide. There were soldiers everywhere. They would have killed us." Manasseh stopped, shame silencing his rambling. He pushed past her and went to the only window in the room. He unlatched the bar and allowed the wooden panels to swing inward. The rain had slackened, the thunder abating. Across the wind-swept streets, clouds threw hesitant shadows. He squinted into the wind toward a distant hill that overshadowed the city. "He's up there. Now. Nailed to that cross. What was I supposed to do? I'm not one of the twelve but I followed Him. I can't fight all of Rome."

Her hands came to rest on his shoulders, warm, reassuring. "I came to tell you there is hope." Manasseh turned to her, and her face was a plane of murky shadows. "I came to tell you there is more. Do not hesitate to believe that one can rise from the dead. Do not give up on Him. He will not give up on you."

Manasseh' heart pounded, and tears swelled in his eyes. "But I let him down! All of His followers did. Even His disciples."

Her smile warmed the room. "There is forgiveness, Manasseh. You will see. Forgiveness and hope."

She turned and started for the door, casting a lingering look around the room. "You've let this house get filthy, Manasseh and I've been gone only two weeks. But, do not despair. There are more important things in life. And, in death."

Manasseh ran to her and stopped as she opened the door. Outside, the wind had ceased, the rain no longer fell, and sunlight streamed in the alleyway. "Remember that I love you." She whispered, reaching out to touch his lips with hers. "And, there is hope."

She turned and started down the alleyway, leaving him alone in the doorway. With tears in his eyes, Manasseh watched her begin the long walk back to her tomb and clung to the knowledge that death, this day, had been forever defeated.

CHAPTER 23

THE BURIAL CLOTH

Joseph took the body, wrapped it in a clean linen cloth, and placed it
in his own new tomb that he had cut out of the rock. He rolled a big
stone in front of the entrance to the tomb and went away.
  Matthew 27:59-60 (NIV)

Othniel made another check on the scroll in front of him. He looked at the names once again, reading off each one silently in the darkness of the temple. He checked, once again, that he had put a mark by each name. Yes, all was well. A name in every column and beside each name a nice, neat little check. Othniel glanced at the white cloths beside him, each stacked neatly on stone shelves. A burial cloth for every priest. It was his job to keep the cloths neat and proper. He cleaned them once a month. He folded them. He placed them on the shelves and checked that they were in place. One never knew when one of the cloths would be needed. He rolled the scroll and sealed it with wax. Satisfied with another job well done, he tucked it in its box. He wouldn't have to check the robes again for another week.

Picking up the small lamp, Othniel stepped out of the room. He shut the wooden door behind him and sealed it with a wooden latch. As he turned, he was startled to see the two men standing before him.

"Good gentlemen, you startled me."

The two men stood before him, silently. Both were dressed in the long black robes. Othniel had been working here as the clerk for many years. He recognized the men instantly as he held the lamp up to their face.

"Nicodemus and Joseph. How odd to see you here at this time of day. Do you need my services?"

Nicodemus glanced at his partner and Joseph turned back to look at Othniel. "Yes, we do. We have need of a burial cloth."

Othniel felt a sudden pain in his heart and he shook his head sadly. "I'm sorry to hear that. Who in our group has passed away?"

Once again, the look passed between the two men. "You do not need to worry about who it is. We have need of a burial cloth." Nicodemus spoke quietly. He held out his hands and Othniel glanced down at them. They were covered with dried blood.

"Oh my. You're unclean. How can you come in the temple with your hands so bloody and dirty?"

Joseph stepped forward; his face close to Othniel. The lamp light reflected brightly in his eyes. "I have already risked my reputation to do what had to be done today. I do not care anymore about what men think about me. I do not care if you think that we are clean or unclean. We did what we had to do. Now, will you give us a burial cloth?"

Othniel stepped away from them until his back was against the wooden door. "This is most irregular. I cannot give you a burial cloth without knowing who it is for. I have to mark it off the list, don't you understand. Everyone has one cloth assigned to him. It's my job to take of them. I can't just give you a burial cloth."

Nicodemus stepped forward close to Joseph's shoulder. "We do not want to break the rules. But there is a man who is going to be buried and he needs a burial cloth. If need be, you may give him mine."

Othniel glanced back and forth between the two of them. "I'm afraid that just won't do. I can't give him your burial cloth. What will you be buried in? You know you can't replace it. These things are very expensive, and they are specially hand-made for each member of the priesthood."

Joseph reached out and took the lamp from Othniel. "Our Master has taught us that we are to love our enemies and that we are to abhor violence. But I must say that if you do not move out of my way, there may be more than just His blood on our hands."

Othniel glanced at the drying blood on their hands and slid aside to allow the wooden door to be opened. He reached out and took the lamp from Joseph.

"Well if you're determined to do this, at least let me make certain that you get the right ones." Othniel stepped into the room beyond and set the lamp on its lamp holder in the side wall. Joseph and Nicodemus crowded into the room with him.

"We'll take this one." Nicodemus reached for a cloth. Othniel's hand snaked out and he stopped the man's arm in mid-reach. Some of the drying blood splattered on his own hand and he glanced at it as if it were acid.

"Let me. Each one of these burial cloths belongs to a specific person. You can't just take any one of them."

Othniel watched as Joseph eyed the piles of cloth. One row of cloths stretched along the lower shelf. There was one shelf above it and on the highest shelf there was a single burial cloth, folded neatly in a stack. Joseph's hand reached out in front of Othniel. "Whose burial cloth is that one."

Othniel glanced at it and he felt spiky cold spear of fear in his heart. "Why, that's the cloth of Caiaphas, the high priest. It's the most special burial cloth in this room."

Without hesitation, Joseph reached up and snared it, the blood leaving little trails of red crimson on the cloth.

"You can't take that cloth!" Othniel was livid with anger. "It's not meant for anybody but the high priest."

Joseph and Nicodemus stepped through the door and Nicodemus turned as Joseph disappeared beyond him. "Do not worry, Othniel. It will be used by the Highest Priest." They disappeared into the darkness.

CHAPTER 24

GUARDIANS OF THE DEAD

The next day, the one after Preparation Day, the chief priests and the Pharisees went to Pilate. "Sir," they said, "we remember that while he was still alive that deceiver said, 'After three days I will rise again.' So give the order for the tomb to be made secure until the third day. Otherwise, his disciples may come and steal the body and tell the people that he has been raised from the dead. This last deception will be worse than the first."

"Take a guard," Pilate answered. "Go, make the tomb as secure as you know how." So they went and made the tomb secure by putting a seal on the stone and posting the guard.

Matthew 27:62-66 (NIV)

"*P*rocutus, wake up! You let the fire die."

The Roman soldier slumped against the rock jerked awake and looked around in confusion. "What?"

"Procutus, I leave for one hour to get us provisions and you fall asleep?" The older Roman soldier said.

Procutus rolled his eyes and ran a hand through his short

hair. "Marcus, the man is dead! He's been dead for a long time and nothing has happened."

Procutus placed a cloth bag and a flagon of wine on the rock beside the younger soldier. "Where is your helmet?"

"I took it off."

"That is one reason you fell asleep." Marcus sat on the rock by the bag. He glanced over his shoulder at the stone rolled before the mouth of a tomb. "Have you forgotten the penalty for failing to do our duty?"

Procutus shrugged and started digging through the bag. "These are confusing times, Marcus."

Marcus jerked the bag away from the younger soldier. "Stoke the fire so we can see. And, put your helmet on and I'll let you have breakfast."

Procutus swore and plopped his plumed helmet on his head. "Marcus, dawn is coming and we can see just fine. It's not that cold for a fire. Besides, the firewood is across the way."

Marcus' wrinkled face shifted in a scowl. "You young people! You have no respect for authority. You don't trust the emperor."

"I don't trust this King Herod, Pilate's puppet. He's the one whose people stirred up all this nonsense about a future king who might come back from the dead."

Marcus pulled bread from the bag along with dried beef. He handed the sack to Procutus. "I remember when the road to Jerusalem was lined with crosses during a rebellion. One of the Herods supported slaughtering his own people. Frankly, I've lost track of who is who." He bit into the beef and chewed. "These criminals all claim to be future kings. They all claim to want to overthrow the emperor. They all claim to have their God's blessing. And, they all have died just as painfully as their fellow criminals. All at the hand of a King Herod."

Procutus bit into the bread. "Then, why are we here? Why are we even bothering to guard the tomb of a dead king? What do they call him?"

"Messiah. We are here because we have been ordered to be here."

"At least we will have relief once the sun is up. I'm looking forward to collapsing in my bed for hours." He drank from the flagon.

"You're going nowhere. We have been ordered to stay until noon."

Procutus shot to his feet. "What? No! I am tired of this place! Tired of these creepy cave tombs. Tired of these superstitious Judeans!"

Marcus stood slowly. "If you desert your post, you will be flogged." He motioned to the tomb. "He was flogged. Brought to the brink of death by the lictors. You know Tiberius?"

"Yeah, he's one of the best." Marcus blinked and rubbed his shoulders. "He's a bit of a sadist. Enjoys his job a little too much."

"Do you want to fall under his cat of nine tails?" Marcus moved closer.

"No." Procutus glanced at the cave. "I heard he was already dead after only six hours."

Marcus nodded. "No need to break his legs like they did the thieves on either side."

"Why'd he die so quickly?" Procutus sat on a rock facing the tomb.

"Some said he sweat blood in the Garden of Gethsemane right before he was arrested. Then, Herod's guards beat him. Then, he came before Pilate and was flogged. I heard he couldn't even carry his cross up the hill." Marcus finished his bread. He swallowed wine.

"He was a weakling, then? A coward?" Procutus spat toward the tomb. "Hardly worth the name of a conquering king, right? Hardly worth the tomb of a rich religious leader, right? And, hardly worth the effort of guarding his tomb. If he died that quickly and was already dead, do they suspect he's only passed out and will recover, roll away that massive stone and walked out of the tomb?"

Marcus regarded Procutus with a weary stare. "So young. So naïve. Procutus, flogging alone would have killed him. He was already the walking dead when they put him under his cross. It's a wonder he was able to walk up the hill at all. I will remind you that our fellow comrades who perform crucifixions must always make sure the victim is dead or they risk taking his place. No, he was quite dead." Marcus looked at the tomb. "Overkill, if you ask me. But his own people demanded he be crucified. It happens all the time."

"What happens?"

Marcus kept his gaze on the tomb. "These so called Messiahs make a promise they can't keep and the people turn against them. It's the way of all humanity. We all eventually turn against ourselves."

Voices echoed out of the waning darkness. Procutus shot to his feet and put a hand on his sword. "Who goes there?"

Out of the shadows a small group of women appeared. The oldest of the women put a hand to her mouth and the other two women reached out to her. One of the women came forward.

"I am Mary and we have come to anoint the body."

"Get your hand off of your sword, Procutus." Marcus said. He rose slowly to his feet. "I'm sorry but we are here to guard the tomb and we cannot allow anyone to open it."

Mary looked back over her shoulder at the older woman. "We will come back later, then."

She turned and the women disappeared into the shadows. "Who did they think would roll the stone away?" Procutus laughed nervously. "Us?"

Marcus rolled his eyes. "Would you relax. It's just women. When they return, and they will after dawn, we'll tell them they have to find someone to open the tomb. That will take time and by then, our relief will have arrived."

The sun peeked over the horizon and the first rays of sunlight hit Procutus in the face. He flinched and put up a hand. "Thank Jupiter it's morning already. Just a few more hours."

The light played across the stone and the earth began to shake. Marcus looked around as nearby bushes trembled and rocks rolled away down the slope. "What is this?"

"An earthquake!" Procutus fell to his knees. "Just like at the crucifixions!"

Marcus leaned against a nearby boulder as the trembling worsened. He glanced over his shoulder at the stone before the tomb. Suddenly, a flash of silent lightning shot down from the clear sky and struck the stone in the center. Marcus fell to his knees. They both looked up at the stone and in the lightning, something formed; a shape, a man in a shining bright robe. Marcus fell back, paralyzed with unreasonable fear. Procutus fell over onto his side, his muscles useless.

The being in white had shining white hair and pale skin with piercing green eyes. He nodded at them and placed a very human appearing hand on the stone. It rolled away of its own accord and the sunlight poured into the mouth of the tomb.

Procutus tried to scream and his mouth would not work. He tried to close his eyes, but they would not close. Something moved inside the tomb. A second figure in glowing white similar to the first walked out and took his place at the opposite side of the tomb entrance from the first man.

Then, He came forward. He wore a simple white robe. His skin was flushed with flowing blood and his lungs moved with air as he paused at the entrance to the tomb. Procutus could not move his head but out of the periphery of his vision he watched the now very much alive carpenter from Bethlehem walk past his motionless body. He noted the wounds in his feet were still there!

Marcus could not see what was happening behind him. He watched as the women returned, huddled in fear. They must have felt the earthquake and seen the lightning from the sky. One of the women moved toward the tomb.

She was shaken and tears poured down her cheeks. When she saw the men behind him at the tomb entrance, she put a hand to her mouth. Her gaze went to Marcus briefly and then back to the tomb. She gasped and disappeared from his sight as she entered the tomb. She ran back into his sight and moaned and sobbed.

Marcus heard the voice of one of the men and it carried the echo of gentle thunder.

"Do not be afraid, for I know that you are looking for Jesus, who was crucified. He is not here; he has risen, just as he said. Come and see the place where he lay. Then go quickly and tell his disciples: 'He has risen from the dead and is going ahead of you into Galilee. There you will see him.' Now I have told you."

The woman hurried past Marcus and the women huddled together. They whispered among themselves.

"I will stay here while you go get the disciples." The woman said. "Take Mary with you. I know this is frightening for her."

"I am not afraid." The older woman said. "He is my son."

The other women took Mary gently by the arm and they disappeared down the trail.

One of the men by the tomb appeared mysteriously at Mary's side. He spoke and his voice was light gentle thunder. "Woman, why are you crying?"

"They have taken my Lord away," she said, "and I don't know where they have put him."

The man in the glowing white robe gestured over Mary's shoulder and then walked away. Behind her, He moved out of the shadows, out of the waning darkness into the full light of a new dawn. Marcus swallowed hard as the man who had walked from the tomb, the man who was dead three days now walked up behind Mary. She sensed his presence and whirled at the sound of his voice.

"Woman, why are you crying? Who is it you are looking for?" He said gently, quietly. Marcus felt tears trickle down his cheek. How could this be? The man was dead! Roman soldiers do not take anyone down from a cross unless they know he is dead, or they would take the victim's place! And yet, here he was walking and talking.

"Good sir, I know you are but the gardener, but I have come for our lord. Sir, if you have carried him away, tell me where you have put him, and I will get him."

"Mary." An unearthly power filled his voice and his face almost glowed!

Mary gasped and fell to her knees. "Rabboni!" She reached out her hands to touch his feet and the man stepped back.

Gasps of wonder came from the other women as they had hurried back up the path. The older woman paused and put a hand to her mouth. "My son!"

Jesus of Nazareth turned slowly and smiled. "Greetings," he said. "Do not be afraid. Go and tell my brothers to go to Galilee; there they will see me." The older woman came forward and fell to her knees, reaching for Jesus' feet.

"Do not hold on to me, for I have not yet ascended to the Father. Go instead to my brothers and tell them, 'I am ascending to my Father and your Father, to my God and your God.'"

The women rose and gathering the younger Mary, backed away quickly, laughing and smiling.

"He is risen!" The older Mary said quietly. They disappeared down the path leaving the risen Jesus standing in the opening before the empty tomb. He turned and cast one lingering look on Marcus. His eyes held the fires of every star, of galaxies formed and dying, of light and life, of love and forgiveness and his gaze burned through Marcus' brain bathing his soul in divine water. Marcus gasped as his muscles responded to his commands. He stood shakily to his feet and watched as Jesus walked away toward the city of Jerusalem.

He turned and the two men in white were gone. All that remained was an empty tomb and his comrade still paralyzed in the dirt. The world, no the universe, had changed forever!

CHAPTER 25

THE BRIBE

While the women were on their way, some of the guards went into the city and reported to the chief priests everything that had happened. When the chief priests had met with the elders and devised a plan, they gave the soldiers a large sum of money, telling them, "You are to say, 'His disciples came during the night and stole him away while we were asleep.' If this report gets to the governor, we will satisfy him and keep you out of trouble." So the soldiers took the money and did as they were instructed. And this story has been widely circulated among the Jews to this very day.

John 20:1-18 (NIV)

*M*arcus glanced across the courtyard and swore. He hobbled across the open courtyard and up onto the portico where Procutus stood nervously.

"Procutus, what are you doing here at the High Priest's residence? I told you to meet me at headquarters."

Procutus glared at him. "I'm not about to tell *them* what

happened! We'd be strung up on crosses just like, just like, HIM! Only we won't walk out of our tombs on the third day."

Marcus sighed. "Procutus, we were sent by Pilate to appease these men in this very house. It's not like we violated Roman law."

"Oh, and who will be the laughingstock after the rest of them find out we let a dead man get up and walk out of his tomb." Procutus hissed.

"Not to mention the angels."

"Don't say that!" Procutus stepped toward him. "They were not angels!"

"Then what were they? Ghosts? Evil spirits?" Marcus sighed. "Let's go before these fanatics find out the body is missing."

"The body is missing?" A short, rotund man stepped through the door. He blinked in the bright morning sunlight and brushed crumbs from his beard. "You interrupted my breakfast."

"He's gone!" Procutus blurted.

The man stiffened and slowly lifted his gaze from his beard to Procutus. "What?"

"The tomb is empty. The stone rolled away and he got up and walked out."

The man glanced at Marcus. "Is this true?"

Marcus nodded. "Two angels came down from heaven and rolled the stone away. We were paralyzed and unable to do anything."

The man's eyes popped from his head and he turned and rushed back into the room. Voices echoed from within and soon a tall, older man in gray robes hurried out onto the porch followed by a dozen men in black robes. "I am Kish, assistant to the high priest. What deceit is this?"

"We're not lying." Procutus said. "Why would we lie?"

"Kish," Marcus said firmly. "We represent the Roman Empire. We represent the real power in this region. Do not accuse of us of lying."

Kish's face reddened, and he stepped back. "He was overheard claiming he would rise from the dead. Don't you see what this means? If this rumor gets circulated, there will be chaos. People will seek him out. They will want to proclaim him king."

"The same ones who called for his crucifixion?" Marcus said.

Kish stuttered and nodded. "True, true. My point is, mobs are unpredictable. Governor Pilate doesn't want a riot on his hands. And, I am certain the Emperor does not want a Judean to proclaim himself king!" Kish nodded and gasped. "Or, Herod, either for that matter."

One of his followers motioned for Kish and whispered in his ear. Kish nodded. "We have reached an agreement. It is important this rumor be quashed."

"It's not a rumor!" Procutus said. "I was there. I saw it all! I saw him walk out of the tomb."

"I have a solution." Kish said quietly. "You are to say, 'His disciples came during the night and stole him away while we were asleep.' If this report gets to the governor, we will satisfy him and keep you out of trouble."

"While we were asleep?" Procutus said. "We will be punished for falling asleep."

"Say they put something in your wine. Drugged you." Kish raised his hands as if this was the ultimate solution.

Marcus stepped between Procutus and Kish. "You're asking us to lie to our own Governor."

"We are prepared to make it worth your while." Kish raised his eyebrows and snapped his fingers. The whispering man placed a sizable leather pouch in Kish's hand. The sound of coins jingled from the bag. "Enough here for each of you to start your own business. Start the rumor and then quietly disappear."

Procutus studied the bag. "That's a lot of money, Marcus."

"Yes, it is. A lot of money to buy a lie."

Procutus took the bag from Kish. "There were other witnesses besides us. They might need a little incentive also."

Kish glanced over his shoulder at his assistant. "Others?"

"Women. They had come to anoint the body." Marcus said.

Kish's mouth twisted into a grin. "Women, you say." He started laughing. "No one will believe the testimony of a woman! They will need no incentive. Their own words will condemn them. So, we have an agreement?"

"Yes!" Marcus took Procutus by the arm and steered him off the porch. He looked back once and saw the entire group of black robed men perched on the porch like a pack of vultures.

"Marcus, that's a lot of money. I don't know if I can lie to Pilate." Procutus said.

Marcus handed the bag to Procutus. He took off his helmet and tossed it aside. He unhitched his sword belt and let it drop to the ground. He shrugged out of his breast plates.

"What are you doing?"

Marcus stretched and now wore only his tunic and sandals. "You are going to do exactly as Kish told you. And, then one day, someone will ask you if you were paid to do so. THEN, you can tell the truth."

Procutus glanced down at Marcus' discarded equipment. "And, why are you doing this?"

"I'm going after the man who rose from the dead. If what we saw is true, and I witnessed it firsthand, then all the money in the world means nothing from now on. You are young. You can't afford to hang your life on a whim. Do your job. Start the rumor. If what this man says is true and there is a resurrection, then no manner of lie will cover the truth. Goodbye, Procutus."

Marcus walked away from the High Priest's house and his armor to find a New Life.

CHAPTER 26

THE CARPENTER'S BROTHER — PART 2

For what I received I passed on to you as of first importance: that Christ died for our sins according to the Scriptures, that he was buried, that he was raised on the third day according to the Scriptures, and that he appeared to Cephas, and then to the Twelve. After that, he appeared to more than five hundred of the brothers and sisters at the same time, most of whom are still living, though some have fallen asleep. Then he appeared to James, then to all the apostles, and last of all he appeared to me also, as to one abnormally born.

1 Corinthians 15:3-8 (NIV)

The news reached me this morning. I came to Jerusalem for the Passover and to visit Mother. The others stayed behind. I knew about the tumult in the streets. I heard about the arrest of my brother.

But I did nothing. After all, he brought this on himself. If he had listened to me before now and had declared himself at the

Feast, he would have been lauded, welcomed as a hero. Or, fittingly enough, denounced as a madman and this crazy crusade of his would have ended. He could have come home to Mother and taken my place in the carpenter's shop.

Yes, there was no reason for me to feel guilty. What had I done wrong? True, my tongue often has gotten me into trouble. It is a terrible creature that rules my life and steers me into so much trouble like a rudder with its own mind! And now, he has died and left his followers tossed in the wind to the four corners of the earth. Every miracle he supposedly performed is now null and void. Every maxim he taught will soon be forgotten. Every life he touched will now revert back to our ordinary, mundane existence.

Like this tiny lamp in my dark room, his meaning, his purpose, his existence was wiped out like blowing out the lamp. Darkness descended on us before he died and the hope and forgiveness he tried to bring to this world is now lost and meaningless. Much like our very existence.

Son of God! Such arrogance! Such hubris! Listen to me. I sound like one of the Pharisees. I might as well serve on the court of the High Priest! Mother would not approve of my opinions. But, if he was so powerful, if he had a mission from God, if he was truly the Messiah, then his death ended the dream! It is over. The rest of us brothers are just plain old ordinary folk without delusions of godhood.

Wait! What is that? A knock at the door? My heart raced with fear. Would the authorities come after his brothers? Were we in the same category as his followers? Must I denounce him again?

I moved to the door and breathed a silent prayer for protection. After all, now that Jesus was gone it would be up to me to take care of Mother. Someone has to take care of the widows and orphans! That would be true religious devotion! Not devotion to a lost cause! I could not afford to go to prison, or worse, hang on a cross. Nothing could make me take the martyr's path!

I opened the door and the bright noonday sun poured into my room. A sudden wind blew out the lamp light and the man standing before me was silhouetted against the light. I squinted against the brightness and stepped back into the room, hands up in defense.

"Who is it? If you're with the Romans, I am not one of his followers. I am but his brother and I tried to stop him."

The man was silent and the stepped into the room. He crossed to the table and suddenly the lamp was lit again! He lifted the tiny lamp from my meager table, a table Jesus and I had made with father's help. He ran a hand over the smooth surface of the table, and I saw the wounds on the back of his hand! He lifted the lamp to his chest and light filled his face, illuminated his eyes, outlined the wounds on his brow. Those eyes! I had looked into them a thousand times but never had they so penetrated to my very soul! It was Jesus! He was alive!

"My brother, you are alive?" I gasped in terror and wonder. The threads of the tapestry dangling in the wind, blowing asunder in confusion came together in sudden clarity. Could it be? Was my brother the true Messiah? The threads wove together in my mind forming a seamless tapestry of God the father, the Son, and his holy presence within, the Spirit. I had heard most of the sermons and had disregarded them as empty promises. But, if my brother had truly overcome death; if He was the Messiah, the Savior, then everything he had said, everything he had done came together in a cohesive whole. I saw the prophecies of the Scriptures like veins in the wood moving toward epiphany, toward convergence.

Before me stood Completion, the perfect lamb of God sacrificed for us all. Would that include me? The brother who had defied Him? The brother whose anger and strident voice had condemned Him as a madman? I had once thought He must have been a lunatic or a liar. But, now, I realized He was Lord! I fell to my knees and the world, the universe changed. No, the universe and all of time and space made total sense of reality.

"My Lord!" I said.

CHAPTER 27

THE FINAL TABLE

Now that same day two of them were going to a village called Emmaus, about seven miles from Jerusalem. They were talking with each other about everything that had happened. As they talked and discussed these things with each other, Jesus himself came up and walked along with them; but they were kept from recognizing him.

He asked them, "What are you discussing together as you walk along?"

They stood still, their faces downcast. One of them, named Cleopas, asked him, "Are you the only one visiting Jerusalem who does not know the things that have happened there in these days?"

"What things?" he asked.

"About Jesus of Nazareth," they replied. "He was a prophet, powerful in word and deed before God and all the people. The chief priests and our rulers handed him over to be sentenced to death, and they crucified him; but we had hoped that he was the one who was going to redeem Israel. And what is more, it is the third day since all this took place. In addition, some of our women amazed us. They went to the tomb early this morning but didn't find his body. They came and told us that they had seen a vision of angels, who said he was

*alive. Then some of our companions went to the tomb and found it
just as the women had said, but they did not see Jesus."*

*He said to them, "How foolish you are, and how slow to believe all
that the prophets have spoken! Did not the Messiah have to suffer
these things and then enter his glory?" And beginning with Moses and
all the Prophets, he explained to them what was said in all the
Scriptures concerning himself.*

*As they approached the village to which they were going, Jesus
continued on as if he were going farther. But they urged him strongly,
"Stay with us, for it is nearly evening; the day is almost over." So he
went in to stay with them.*

*When he was at the table with them, he took bread, gave thanks,
broke it and began to give it to them. Then their eyes were opened and
they recognized him, and he disappeared from their sight. They asked
each other, "Were not our hearts burning within us while he talked
with us on the road and opened the Scriptures to us?"*

*They got up and returned at once to Jerusalem. There they found
the Eleven and those with them, assembled together and saying, "It is
true! The Lord has risen and has appeared to Simon." Then the two
told what had happened on the way, and how Jesus was recognized by
them when he broke the bread.*

Luke 24:13-35 (NIV)

"*W*here are you going Josiah?"

I looked up from my wine at the proprietor
of this little inn. We had known each other for years only the
distance of his inn from Jerusalem being the limitation to our
friendship.

"I'm going back to Bethlehem. Too many horrible things are
happening in Jerusalem." I drank more wine hoping the
growing numbness inside would engulf me.

"Where is Rachel? Isn't she going with you?"

"Obed, I'm going ahead to see if we can purchase back our old inn. If all goes as planned, she will join me."

Obed sat across the table from me, wiping his hands on a towel. His graying beard was dotted with breadcrumbs. "And what of your daughter, your grandchildren, your son?"

My heart skipped a beat and I looked away as the anger mixed with sorrow rose like bile within my throat. "Joseph is dead. Crucified. Like my brother."

Obed groaned and put his face in his hands. "No! I remember your brother Joseph. He was a hot-headed rebel."

"So was my son." I guzzled more wine. "I can't stay there anymore, Obed. The pain is too great."

"So, you're running away?" He looked at me with wet eyes.

"Yes. I am running away as quickly as I can."

Obed glanced up as three men entered the inn. "There's nowhere you can run to escape the problems of this world, Josiah." He stood slowly and welcomed the three men and showed them to a table.

I ignored their excited conversation and tried to focus on the numbing feeling of the wine. I had miles to go before I could sleep in my hometown, but for now getting twenty or so miles away from Jerusalem would have to suffice.

"So, you're saying that the Messiah's coming is all part of the fulfillment of the prophecies?" One of the men asked.

"That's exactly what he is saying, Cleopus. I see it now! We thought the Messiah was a conquering king. But that is not the picture the scriptures have painted of him. Imagine, a servant king who comes to die as the ultimate sacrifice for our sins. And, not just a king, but the King of Kings! The true son of God!"

The third man at the table arose and walked to the far door and disappeared outside. "Where is he going?" I found himself asking as I turned to face the two men.

"He'll be back shortly. Who are you?"

"I am Josiah. I was there when this Messiah was nailed to a cross. Were you some of his followers?"

Cleopus motioned me to join them. I brought my wine and sat at their table. "We were no close disciples. We followed from afar. Some of us where afraid to commit. You see, we believed Jesus of Nazareth was a prophet, powerful in word and deed before God and all the people. The chief priests and our rulers handed him over to be sentenced to death, and they crucified him; but we had hoped that he was the one who was going to redeem Israel. And what is more, it is the third day since all this took place."

The other man nodded. "In addition, some of our women amazed us. They went to the tomb early this morning but didn't find his body. They came and told us that they had seen a vision of angels, who said he was alive. Then some of our companions went to the tomb and found it just as the women had said, but they did not see Jesus."

"It made no sense until our companion met us on the road to Emmaus and you know what he said? 'How foolish you are, and how slow to believe all that the prophets have spoken! Did not the Messiah have to suffer these things and then enter his glory?' And then, beginning with Moses and all the Prophets, he explained to us what was said in all the Scriptures concerning himself. He opened our eyes to the true meaning of the scriptures."

I felt my heart race. The events I had witnessed at the cross had left me with no doubt the carpenter of Bethlehem was the true Messiah. But, he had died and had been sealed in a tomb. He was dead, gone. But, if it was true and he had come back from the dead, it changed everything.

"Then, if he is the Son of God and if he rose from the dead, then this world will never be the same. We no longer have to fear death!"

Cleopus nodded and laughed. "Yes! And, I am becoming convinced this is true."

A shadow fell over me and I looked at the silhouette of the third man. He had returned from outside. He held a cup in one hand and a loaf of bread in the other. His eyes met mine though his face was obscured by shadow.

The man placed the bread and cup on the table. He took the bread and broke it into pieces and passed a piece to each of us. I took the bread and looked at it with confusion. The man then lifted his piece of bread to his mouth. "This is my body with is broken for the remission of sin. Eat all of it."

His voice was so commanding, so comforting, so powerful as if the mountains had spoken and sea had laughed back in joy. Something came over me, a wave of peace and contentment I had not felt in years.

The man lifted the cup and held it up into a stray ray of sunshine. I looked around the inn. Everyone had frozen, eyes fixed on the man with the cup. "This is my blood shed for the remission of sins. Drink all of it."

He passed the cup to Cleopus who sipped it and passed it to his companion. His companion took a sip and passed it to me.

I lifted the cup to my lips with trembling hands. Body broken. Blood shed. Like a lamb led to slaughter. In a wave of cold awareness, it all fell into place. I drank the bitter wine and felt it coat my mouth and course down my throat. I handed the cup to the man and when the man took it, I gasped at the sight of the wounds in his palm and wrist.

I stood slowly just as Cleopus and his companion arose in equal surprise.

"Master!" Cleopus said and fell to his knees. His companion did likewise. Their sobs filled the quiet air. My gaze met the powerful gaze of the Son of God, Prince of Peace, King of Kings, the Christ. He had risen! It was true. I had been gifted among all men to have seen the Savior from birth to death to new life! I slowly crumpled to my knees, my eyes filling with tears of joy. Christ was risen indeed and nothing would ever be the same!

EPILOGUE

ENLIGHTENED BY THE BLIND

*S*imeon heard a noise and the door to his house burst open. He sat upright on his pallet, his eyes still filled with sleep, as the bright sunlight gushed into the room. A figure stood in the doorway, eclipsing the sunlight.

"Who's there?"

The figure remained silent, silhouetted against the bright light and he stepped into the room. Motes of dust swirled in the air, as the man stepped up to the pallet and looked down at Simeon.

Simeon stood slowly and squinted at the man's face. The man was dressed in rich, royal robes with gold chains around his neck and he wore an expensive headdress. His face was very severe, dark, with glistening eyes and a jet-black beard. A finger covered with jeweled rings pointed in accusation and Simeon was pushed roughly in the chest back against the stone wall of his bedroom.

"Are you Simeon, the Christian?" The man's harsh voice echoed in the room.

Simeon stumbled against the wall and then regained his

composure. "I am Simeon, he who follows Christ. Yes. Who are you?"

The man turned and glanced toward the outer doorway and Simeon saw two soldiers standing in the bright sunlight outside. "I have come to take you away. You are a follower of that blasphemer Christ and if you do not denounce him, you will be put to death."

Simeon swallowed nervously and stepped beyond the man to the small table in his room. From a gourd he poured a cup of water and sipped the water as he glanced towards the doorway. Two Judean soldier stood outside his doorway. Already a small crowd was gathering in the morning sunlight. He turned and the man who had accosted him was facing the doorway, the bright sunlight glistening from his jewelry and gold chains.

"Just who are you?"

"I am Saul of Tarsus. It is my job to root out this evil cult, which is growing in this community, in this nation."

The wooden cup fell from Simeon's hand and clattered on the tabletop, splashing water across the room. Small droplets of it landed on Saul's face and glistened in the sunlight.

"You were responsible for Steven's death, weren't you?"

Saul wiped the droplets from his face and glanced at his hand. "Yes. I was responsible for the death of that blasphemer. You too will suffer a similar fate. You must denounce this Jesus Christ. You must denounce that you were ever involved in his teaching and his miracles. If you do so publicly, then I will spare your life."

Simeon looked around the small room in which he had lived for the last few years. "I have never married. I have spent my days teaching and spreading the news of Jesus Christ, just as my master had instructed me to do on the day of his departure into the heavens. As you can see, I have very few earthly possessions." He gestured to the empty and bare room, testimony to a life lived without material possessions. "I may not have many

possessions, but my heart is filled with the riches and the treasures of souls saved for Jesus Christ. Those things could never
be taken from me." He straightened and smiled.

"Saul of Tarsus, I must tell you that I was once blind. I lived
the life of a beggar, a slave to darkness. And one day Jesus Christ
touched my eyes and healed me, and I not only could see again
physically, but my soul and my heart could see the truth. The
truth is that Jesus Christ is the Son of God and that truth has set
me free. I can never denounce him. I can never denounce the
miracle that he performed in my life. If Jesus Christ could pay
for the truth with his own life, then I can do no less. I will not
denounce Him. If I must be put to death at your hands, then so
be it. For I know that just as my Savior and Lord rose again
from the dead, I will live again with Him in eternity."

Saul grimaced. "You Christians are all alike. You're so puny
and weak. And every one of you refuses to denounce this self-
professed messiah, who's leading you into the very pits of
Gehenna. I grow so weary of your presence here. I grow so
weary of your smiling faces and your unyielding devotion to
this Jesus of Nazareth. If I have to, I will chase every one of you
to the very ends of the earth, until I've wiped you out. I shall
have mercy on you today, Simeon. I shall have mercy because I
am a busy man today. I'm about to leave on a long journey to
Damascus. When I arrive, there are a group of Christians who
will die at my hands. But I will return for you. I shall come back
to this house and you shall suffer at my hands."

Simeon looked towards the outer doorway and the sunlight
was full and warm on his face. "Then I shall wait for you Saul. I
shall be here doing what God has commissioned me to do. But I
warn you Saul. You are fighting forces far beyond your understanding. You will have to face Jesus one day, face to face, and
you will have to account for these murders and atrocities. And
when you do, you will see the truth, even as I have. And the
truth will either make you free or will enslave you into eternal

darkness. And it is in our darkness we find His light. Saul of Tarsus, one day you will meet Jesus and you will be blinded by his light. Until that day, I await your return."

Saul glared at him one last time and extended a clinched fist. "I would like to meet this Jesus of yours. And when I do, I would give him a piece of my mind. There is no man, no so called Son of God so powerful that he could change my mind and change my course. Simeon, I will return and when I do, you will die."

Saul brushed past him and paused in the doorway. As he turned the light glistened once more on the fine droplets of water on his face, reflecting from the gold around his neck and the jewels on his hands. "I am not blind Simeon. You are the one who has been blinded by this untruth. When I return from Damascus, I will show you the truth."

Simeon watched as Saul disappeared into the bright morning sunlight. He sat on his pallet and gazed into the rays of the morning sun. "Oh, Master and Savior, I know not what you have in mind for me. But please, today, soften Saul's heart and let him meet you face to face."

On that day a great persecution broke out against the church in Jerusalem, and all except the apostles were scattered throughout Judea and Samaria. Godly men buried Stephen and mourned deeply for him. But Saul began to destroy the church. Going from house to house, he dragged off both men and women and put them in prison.

Acts 8:1-3 (NIV)

ABOUT THE AUTHOR

Bruce Hennigan grew up in Northwest Louisiana and became a physician practicing in the field of radiology. He was a church drama director for 15 years and wrote over 150 plays. He is a certified apologist, or one who defends the truthfulness of the Christian faith and speaks on this topic on a regular basis. Bruce is also the author of six books in the supernatural thriller series, "The Chronicles of Jonathan Steel" as well as "Death by Darwin" and, with Mark Sutton, "Hope Again: A Lifetime Plan for Conquering Depression."

Fiction:
   The 13th Demon: Altar of the Spiral Eye
   The 12th Demon: Mark of the Wolf Dragon
   The 11th Demon: The Ark of Chaos
   The 10th Demon: Children of the Bloodstone
   The 9th Demon: Time of the Cross
   The 8th Demon: A Wicked Numinosity
   Death By Darwin (Featuring the first appearance of Jonathan Steel)
   The Homecoming Tree
   Upcoming:
   The 7th Demon: The Unholy Triad

Non-Fiction:
   Hope Again: A Lifetime Plan for Conquering Depression

IDENTITY

A SMOKE & MIRRORS BOOK

3

A Tale of Murder, Mystery and Romance

H. D. THOMSON